UNCANNY

UNCANNY

UNCANNY STORIES AND
MORE UNCANNY STORIES
FROM *THE NOVEL MAGAZINE*

COACHWHIP PUBLICATIONS

Greenville, Ohio

Uncanny: Uncanny Stories and More Uncanny Stories from The Novel Magazine
© 2014 Coachwhip Publications
No claims made on public domain material.
Uncanny Stories published 1916.
More Uncanny Stories published 1918.
(Stories published individually in *The Novel Magazine*.)
Cover: Background © Lost & Taken; Submarine © Keith Bishop

ISBN 1-61646-244-2
ISBN-13 978-1-61646-244-4

CoachwhipBooks.com

CONTENTS

THE UNKNOWN QUANTITY
E. R. PUNSHON

PROFESSOR WILLIAM JAMES MAYNARD was in a singularly happy and contented mood as he strolled down the High Street after a long and satisfactory interview with the solicitor to his late cousin, whose sole heir he was.

It was exactly a month by the calendar since he had murdered this cousin, and everything had gone most satisfactorily since. The fortune was proving quite as large as he had expected, and not even an inquest had been held upon the dead man. The coroner had decided that it was not necessary, and the Professor had agreed with him.

At the funeral the Professor had been the principal mourner, and the local paper had commented sympathetically on his evident emotion. This had been quite genuine, for the Professor had been fond of his relative, who had always been very good to him. But still, when an old man remains obstinately healthy, when his doctor can say with confidence that he is good for another twenty years at least, and when he stands between you and a large fortune which you need, and of which you can make much better use in the cause of science and the pursuit of knowledge, what alternative is there? It becomes necessary to take steps. Therefore, the Professor had taken steps.

Looking back to-day on that day a month ago, and the critical preceding week, the Professor felt that the steps he had taken had been as judicious as successful. He had set himself to solve a problem in higher mathematics. He had found it easier to solve than many he was obliged to grapple with in the course of his studies.

A policeman saluted as the Professor passed, and he acknowledged it with the charming old world courtesy that made him so popular a figure in the town. Across the way was the doctor who had certified the cause of death. The Professor, passing benevolently on, was glad he had now enough money to carry out his projects. He would be able to publish at once his great work on "The Secondary Variation of the Differential Calculus," that hitherto had languished in manuscript. It would make a sensation, he thought; there was more than one generally accepted theory he had challenged or contradicted in it. And he would put in hand at once his great, his long projected work, "A History of the Higher Mathematics." It would take twenty years to complete, it would cost twenty thousand pounds or more, and it would breathe into mathematics the new, vivid life that Bergson's works have breathed into metaphysics.

The Professor thought very kindly of the dead cousin, whose money would provide for this great work. He wished greatly the dead man could know to what high use his fortune was designed.

Coming towards him he saw the wife of the vicar of his parish. The Professor was a regular church-goer. The vicar's wife saw him, too, and beamed. She and her husband were more than a little proud of having so well known a man in their congregation. She held out her hand and the Professor was about to take it when she drew it back with a startled movement.

"Oh, I beg your pardon!" she exclaimed, distressed, as she saw him raise his eyebrows. "There is blood on it."

Her eyes were fixed on his right hand, which he was still holding out. In fact, on the palm a small drop of blood showed distinctly against the firm, pink flesh. Surprised, the Professor took out his handkerchief and wiped it away. He noticed that the vicar's wife was wearing white kid gloves.

"Oh, I beg your pardon!" she said again. "It—it startled me somehow. I thought you must have cut yourself. I hope it's not much?"

"Some scratch, I suppose," he said. "It's nothing."

The vicar's wife, still slightly discomposed, launched out into some parochial matter she had wished to mention to him. They chatted a few moments and then parted. The Professor took an

8

opportunity to look at his hand. He could detect no sign of any cut or abrasion, the skin seemed whole everywhere. He looked at his handkerchief. There was still visible on it the stain where he had wiped his hand, and this stain seemed certainly blood.

"Odd!" he muttered as he put the handkerchief back in his pocket. "Very odd!"

His thoughts turned again to his projected "A History of the Higher Mathematics," and he forgot all about the incident till, as it happened that day month, the first of the month by the calendar, when he was sitting in his study with an eminent colleague to whom he was explaining his great scheme.

"If you are able to carry it out," the colleague said slowly, "your book will mark an epoch in human thought. But the cost will be tremendous."

"I estimate it at twenty thousand pounds," answered the Professor calmly. "I am fully prepared to spend twice as much. You know I have recently inherited forty thousand pounds from a relative?"

The eminent colleague nodded and looked very impressed.

"It is magnificent," he said warmly, "magnificent." He added: "You've cut yourself, do you know?"

"Cut myself?" the Professor echoed, surprised.

"Yes," answered the eminent colleague, "there is blood upon your hand—your right hand."

In fact a spot of blood, slightly larger than that which had appeared before, showed plainly upon the Professor's right hand. He wiped it away with his handkerchief, and went on talking eagerly, for he was deeply interested. He did not think of the matter again till just as he was getting into bed, when he noticed a red stain upon his handkerchief. He frowned and examined his hand carefully. There was no sign of any wound or cut from which the blood could have come, and he frowned again.

"Very odd!" he muttered.

A calendar hanging on the wall reminded him that it was the first of the month.

The days passed, the incident faded from his memory, and four weeks later he came down one morning to breakfast in an unusually good temper. There was a certain theory he had worked on the night before he meant to write to a friend about. It seemed to him his demonstration had been really brilliant, and then, also, he was already planning out with great success the details of the scheme for his great work.

He was making an excellent breakfast, for his appetite was always good, and, needing some more cream, he rang the bell. The maid appeared, he showed her the empty jug, and as she took it she dropped it with a sudden cry, smashing it to pieces on the floor. Very pale, she stammered out:

"Beg pardon, sir, your hand—there is blood upon your hand."

In fact, on the Professor's right hand there showed a drop of blood, perceptibly larger this time than before. The Professor stared at it stupidly. He was sure it had not been there a moment before, and he noticed by the heading of the newspaper at the side of his plate that this was the first of the month.

With a hasty movement of his napkin he wiped the drop of blood away. The maid, still apologising, began to pick up the pieces of the jug she had broken; but the Professor had no further appetite for his breakfast. He silenced her with a gesture, and, leaving a piece of toast half-eaten on his plate, he got up and went into his study.

All this was trivial, absurd even. Yet somehow it disturbed him. He got out a magnifying glass and examined his hand under it. There was nothing to account for the presence of the drop of blood he and the maid had seen. It occurred to him that he might have cut himself in shaving; but when he looked in the mirror he could find no trace of even the slightest wound.

He decided that, though he had not been aware of it, his nerves must be a little out of order. That was disconcerting. He had not taken his nerves into consideration for the simple reason that he had never known that he possessed any. He made up his mind to treat himself to a holiday in Switzerland. One or two difficult ascents might brace him up a bit.

Three days later he was in Switzerland, and a few days later again he was on the summit of a minor but still difficult peak. It had been an exhilarating climb, and he had enjoyed it. He said something laughingly to the head guide to the effect that climbing was good sport and a fine test for the nerves. The head guide agreed, and added politely that if the nerves of monsieur the Professor had shown signs of failing on the lower glacier, for example, they might all have been in difficulties. The Professor thrilled with pleasure at the head guide's implied praise. He was glad to know on such good authority that his nerves were all right, and the incidents that had driven him there began to fade in his memory.

Nevertheless, he found himself watching the calendar with a certain interest, and when he woke on the morning of the first day of the next month he glanced quickly at his right hand. There was nothing there.

He dressed and spent, as he had planned, a quiet day, busy with his correspondence. His spirits rose as the day passed. He was still watchful, but more confident; and, after dinner, though he had meant to go straight to his room, he agreed to join in a suggested game of bridge. They were cutting for partners when one of the ladies who was to take part in the game dropped with a little cry the card she had just lifted.

"Oh, there is blood upon your hand," she cried, "on your right hand, Professor!"

Upon the Professor's right hand there showed now a drop of blood, larger still then those other three had been. Yet the very moment before it had not been there. The Professor put down his cards without a word, and left the room, going straight upstairs.

The drop of blood was still standing on his hand. He soaked it up carefully with some cotton-wool he had, and was not surprised to find beneath no sign or trace of any cut or wound. The cotton-wool he made up carefully into a parcel and addressed it to an analytical chemist he knew, inclosing with it a short note.

He rang the bell, sent the parcel to the post, and then he got out pen and paper and set himself to solve this problem, as in his life he had solved so many others.

Only this time it seemed somehow as though the data were insufficient.

Idly his pen traced upon the paper in front of him a large X, the sign of the unknown quantity.

But how, in this case, to find out what was the unknown quantity? His hand, his firm and steady hand, shook so that he could no longer hold his pen. He rang the bell again and ordered a stiff whisky-and-soda. He was a man of almost ascetic habits, but tonight he felt that he needed some stimulant.

Neither did he sleep very well.

The next day he returned to England. Almost at once he went to see his friend, the analytical chemist, to whom he had sent the parcel from Switzerland.

"Mammalian blood," pronounced the chemist, "probably human—rather a curious thing about it, too."

"What's that?" asked the Professor.

"Why," his friend answered, "I was able to identify the distinctive bacillus—" He named the rare bacillus of an unusual and obscure disease. And this disease was that from which the Professor's cousin had died.

The professor was a man interested in all phenomena. In other circumstances he would have observed keenly that which now occurred, when the hair of his head underwent a curious involuntary stiffening and bristling process that in popular but sufficiently accurate terms, might be described as "standing on end." But at the moment he was in no state for scientific observations.

He got out of the house somehow. He said he did not feel well, and his friend, the chemist, agreed that his holiday in Switzerland did not seem to have done him much good.

The Professor went straight home and shut himself up in his study. It was a fine room, ranged all round with books. On the shelves nearest to his hand stood volumes on mathematics, the theory of mathematics, the study of mathematics, pure mathematics, applied mathematics. But there was not any one of these books that told him anything about such a thing as this. Though, it is true, there were many references in them, here and there, to X, the unknown quantity.

12

The Professor took his pen and wrote a large X upon the sheet of paper in front of him.

"An unknown quantity!" he muttered. "An unknown—quantity!"

The days passed peacefully. Nothing was out of the ordinary except that the Professor developed an odd trick of continually glancing at his right hand. He washed it a good deal, too. But the first of the month was not yet.

On the last day of the month he told his housekeeper that he was feeling a little unwell. She was not surprised, for she had thought him looking ill for some time past. He told her he would probably spend the next day in bed for a thorough rest, and she agreed that that would be a very good idea. When he was in his own room and had undressed, he bandaged his right hand with care, tying it up carefully and thoroughly with three or four of his large linen handkerchiefs.

"Whatever comes, shall now show," he said to himself.

He stayed in bed accordingly the next day. His housekeeper was a little uneasy about him. He ate nothing and his eyes were strangely bright and feverish. She overheard him once muttering something to himself about "the unknown quantity," and that made her think that he had been working too hard.

She decided he must see the doctor. The Professor refused peremptorily. He declared he would be quite well again in the morning. The housekeeper, an old servant, agreed, but sent for the doctor all the same; and when he had come the Professor felt he could not refuse to see him without appearing peculiar. And he did not wish to appear peculiar. So he saw the doctor, but declared there was nothing much the matter, he merely felt a little unwell and out of sorts and tired.

"You have hurt your hand?" the doctor asked, noticing how it was bandaged.

"I cut it slightly—a trifle," the Professor answered.

"Yes," the doctor answered, "I see there is blood on it."

"What?" the Professor stammered.

"There is blood upon your hand," the doctor repeated.

The Professor looked. In fact, a deep, wide stain showed crimson upon the bandages in which he had swathed his hand. Yet he knew that the moment before the linen had been fair and white and clean.

"It is nothing," he said quickly, hiding his hand beneath the bed clothes.

The doctor, a little puzzled, took his leave, but had not gone ten yards when the housekeeper flew screaming after him. It seemed she had heard a fall, and when she had gone into the Professor's bedroom she had found him lying there dead upon the hearthrug. There was a razor in his hand, and there was a ghastly gash across his throat.

The doctor went back at a run, but there was nothing he or any man could do. One thing he noticed, with curiosity, was that the bandage had been torn away from the dead man's hand and that oddly enough there seemed to be on the hand no sign of any cut or wound. There was a large solitary drop of blood on the palm, at the root of the thumb; but, of course, that was no great wonder, for the wound the dead man had dealt himself had bled freely.

Apparently death had not been quite instantaneous, for with a last effort the Professor seemed to have traced an X upon the floor in his own blood with his forefinger. The doctor mentioned this at the inquest—the coroner had decided at once that in this case an inquest was certainly necessary—and he suggested that it showed the Professor had worked too hard and was suffering from overwork which had disturbed his mental balance.

The coroner took the same view, and in his short address to the jury adduced the incident as proof of a passing mental disturbance.

"Very probably," said the coroner, "there was some problem that had worried him, and that he was still endeavouring to work out. As you are aware, gentlemen, the sign X is used to symbolise the unknown quantity."

An appropriate verdict was accordingly returned, and the Professor was duly interred in the same family vault as that in which so short a time previously his cousin had been laid to rest.

THE ARMLESS MAN
W. G. LITT

I FIRST MET BOB MASTERS in the hotel at a place called Fourteen Streams, not very far from Kimberley.

I had for some months been trying to find gold or diamonds by digging holes in the veldt. But since this has little or nothing to do with the story, I pass by my mining adventures and come back to the hotel. I came to it very readily that afternoon, for I was very thirsty.

A tall man standing at the bar turned his head as I entered and said "Good-day" to me. I returned the compliment, but took no particular notice of him at first.

Suddenly I heard the man say to the barman:

"I'm ready for another drink."

That surprised me, because his glass was still three-quarters full. But I was still more startled by the action of the barman who lifted up the glass and held it whilst the man drank.

Then I saw the reason. The man had no arms.

You know the easy way in which Englishmen chum together anywhere out of England, whilst in their native country nothing save a formal introduction will make them acquainted? I made some remark to Masters which led to another from him, and in five minutes' time we were chatting on all sorts of topics.

I learnt that Masters, bound for England, had come in to Fourteen Streams to catch the train from Kimberley, and, having a few hours to wait, had strolled up to the collection of tin huts calling itself a town.

I was going down to Kimberley too, so of course we went together, and were quite old friends by the time we reached that city.

We had a wash and something to eat, and then we walked round to the post-office. I used to have my letters addressed there, *poste restante*, and call in for them when I happened to be in Kimberley.

I found several letters, one of which altered the whole course of my life. This was from Messrs. Harvey, Filson, and Harvey, solicitors, Lincoln's Inn Fields. It informed me that the sudden death of my cousin had so affected my uncle's health that he had followed his only son within the month. The senior branch of the family being thus extinct the whole of the entailed estate had devolved on me.

The first thing I did was to send off two cablegrams to say that I was coming home by the first available boat, one to the solicitors, the other to Nancy Milward.

Masters and I arranged to come home together and eventually reached Cape Town. There we had considerable trouble at the shipping office. It was just about the time of year when people who live in Africa to make money, come over to England to spend it, and in consequence the boats were very crowded. Masters demanded a cabin to himself, a luxury which was not to be had, though there was one that he and I could share. He made a tremendous fuss about doing this, and I thought it very strange, because I had assisted him in many ways which his mutilation rendered necessary. However, he had to give way in the end, and we embarked on the Castle liner.

On the voyage he told me how he had lost his arms. It seemed that he had been sent up country on some Government job or other, and had had the ill-fortune to be captured by the natives. They treated him quite well at first, but gave him to understand that he must not try to escape. I suppose that to most men such a warning would be a direct incitement to make the attempt. Masters made it and failed. They cut off his right arm as a punishment. He waited until the wound was healed and tried again. Again he failed. This time they cut off his other arm.

"Good Lord," I cried. "What devils!"

"Weren't they!" he said. "And yet, you know, they were quite good-tempered chaps when you didn't cross them. I wasn't going to be beaten by a lot of naked niggers though, and I made a third attempt.

"I succeeded all right that time, though, of course, it was much more difficult. I really don't know at all how I managed to worry through. You see, I could only eat plants and leaves and such fruit as I came across; but I'd learnt as much as I could of the local botany in the intervals."

"Was it worth while?" I asked. "I think the first failure and its result would have satisfied me."

"Yes," he said slowly, "it was worth while. You see, my wife was waiting for me at home, and I wanted to see her again very badly— you don't know how badly."

"I think I can imagine," I said. "Because there is a girl waiting for me too at home."

"I saw her before she died," he continued.

"Died?" I said.

"Yes," he answered. "She was dying when I reached home at last, but I was with her at the end. That was something, wasn't it?"

I do hate people to tell me this sort of thing. Not because I do not feel sorry for them; on the contrary, I feel so sorry that I absolutely fail to find words to express my sympathy. I tried, however, to show it in other ways, by the attentions I paid him and by anticipating his every wish.

Yet there were many things that were astonishing about his actions, things that I wonder now I did not realise must have been impossible for him to do for himself, and that yet were done. But he was so surprisingly dexterous with his lips, and feet too, when he was in his cabin that I suppose I put them down to that.

I remember waking up one night and looking out of my bunk to see him standing on the floor. The cabin was only faintly lit by a moonbeam which found its way through the porthole. I could not see clearly, but I fancied that he walked to the door and opened it, and closed it behind him. He did it all very quickly, as quickly as I could have done it. As I say, I was very sleepy, but the sight of the door opening and shutting like that woke me thoroughly. Sitting up I shouted at him.

He heard me and opened the door again, easily, too, much more easily than he seemed to be able to shut it when he saw me looking at him.

"Hullo! Awake, old chap?" he said. "What is it?"

"Er—nothing," I said. "Or rather I suppose I was only half awake; but you seemed to open that door so easily that it quite startled me."

"One does not always like to let others see the shifts to which one has to resort," was all the answer he gave me.

But I worried over it. The thing bothered me, because he had made no attempt to explain.

That was not the only thing I noticed.

Two or three days later we were sitting together on deck. I had offered to read to him. I noticed that he got up out of his chair. Suddenly I saw the chair move. It gave me a great shock, for the chair twisted apparently of its own volition, so that when he sat down again the sunlight was at his back and not in his eyes, as I knew it had been previously. But I reasoned with myself and managed to satisfy myself that he must have turned the chair round with his foot. It was just possible that he could have done so, for it had one of those light wicker-work seats.

We had a lovely voyage for three-quarters of the way, and the sea was as calm as any duck-pond. But that was all altered when we passed Cape Finisterre. I have done a lot of knocking about on the ocean one way and another, but I never saw the Bay of Biscay deserve its reputation better.

I'd much rather see what is going on than be cooped up below, and after lunch I told Bob I was going up on deck.

"I'll only stay there for a bit," I said. "You make yourself comfortable down here."

I filled his pipe, put it in his mouth, and gave him a match; then I left him.

I made my way up and down the deck for a time, clutching hold of everything handy, and rather enjoyed it, though the waves drenched me to the skin.

Presently I saw Masters come out of the companion-way and make his way very skilfully towards me. Of course it was fearfully dangerous for him.

I staggered towards him, and, putting my lips to his ear, shouted to him to go below at once.

"Oh, I shall be all right!" he said, and laughed.

"You'll be drowned—drowned," I screamed. "There was a wave just now that—well, if I hadn't been able to cling on with both hands like grim death, I should have gone overboard. Go below."

He laughed again and shook his head.

And then what I dreaded happened. A vast mountain of green water lifted up its bulk and fell upon us in a ravening cataract. I clutched at Masters, but trying to save him and myself handicapped me badly. The strength of that mass of water was terrible. It seemed to snatch at everything with giant hands, and drag all with it. It tossed a hen-coop high, and carried it through the rails.

I felt the grip of my right hand loosen, and the next instant was carried, still clutching Masters with my left, towards that gap in the bulwark.

I managed to seize the end of the broken rail. It held us for a moment, then gave, and for a moment I hung sheer over the vessel's side.

In that instant I felt fingers tighten on my arm, tighten till they bit into the flesh, and I was pulled back into safety.

Together we staggered back, and got below somehow. I was trembling like a leaf, and the sweat dripped from me. I almost screamed aloud.

It was not that I was frightened of death. I've seen too much of that in many parts of the earth to dread it greatly. It was the thought of those fingers tightening on me where no fingers were.

Masters did not speak a word, nor did I, until we found ourselves in the cabin.

I tore the wet clothes off me and turned my arm to the mirror. I knew I could not have been mistaken when I felt them.

There on the upper arm, above the line of sunburn that one gets from working with sleeves rolled up, there on the white skin showed *the red marks of four slender fingers and a thumb*! I sat down suddenly at sight of them, and pulling open a drawer, found a flask of neat brandy, and gulped it down, emptied it in one gulp.

Then I turned to him and pointed to the marks.

"In God's name, how came these here?" I said. "What—what happened up there on deck?"

He looked at me very gravely.

"I saved you," he said, "or rather I didn't, for I could not. But *she* did."

"What do you mean?" I stammered.

"Let me get these clothes off," he said, "and some dry ones on; and I'll tell you."

Words fail to describe my feelings as I watched the clothes come off him and dry ones go on just as if hands were arranging them.

I sat and shuddered. I tried to close my eyes, but the weird, unnatural sight drew them as a lodestone.

"I'm sorry that you should have had this shock," he said. "I know what it must have been like, though it was not so bad for me when they seemed to come, for they came gradually as time went on."

"What came gradually?" I asked.

"Why, these arms! They're what I'm telling you about. You asked me to tell you, I thought?"

"Did I?" I said. "I don't know what I'm saying or asking. I think I'm going mad, quite mad."

"No," he said, "you're as sane as I am, only when you come across something strange, unique for that matter, you are naturally terrified. Well, it was like this. I told you about my adventures with the niggers up country. That was quite true. They cut off both my arms—you can see the stumps for that matter. And I told you that I came home to find my wife dying. Her heart had always been weak, I'd known that, and it had gradually grown more feeble. There must have been, indeed there was, a strange sort of telepathy between us. She had had fearful attacks of heart failure on both occasions when the niggers had mutilated me, I learnt on comparing notes.

"But I had known too, somehow, that I must escape at all costs. It was the knowledge that made me try again after each failure. I

20

should have gone on trying to escape as long as I had lived, or rather as long as she had lived. I knelt beside her bed and she put out her arms and laid them round my neck.

"'So you have come back to me before I go,' she said. 'I knew you must, because I called you so. But you have been long in coming, almost too long. But I knew I had to see you again before I died.'

"I broke down then. I was sorely tried. No arms even to put round her!

"'Darling, stay with me for a little, only for a little while!' I sobbed.

"She shook her head feebly. 'It is no use, my dear,' she said, 'I must go.'

"'I'll come with you,' I said, 'I'll not live without you.'

"She shook her head again.

"'You must be brave, Bob. I shall be watching you afterwards just as much as if I still lived on earth. If only I could give you my arms! A poor, weak woman's arms, but better than none, dear.'

"She died some weeks later. I spent all the time at her bedside, I hardly left her. Her arms were round me when she died. Shall I ever feel them round me again? I wonder! You see, they are mine now.

"They came to me gradually. It was very strange at first to have arms and hands which one couldn't see. I used to keep my eyes shut as much as possible, and try to fancy that I had never lost my arms.

"I got used to them in time. But I have always been careful not to let people see me do things that they would know to be impossible for an armless man. That was what took me to Africa again, because I could get lost there and do things for myself with these hands."

"'And they twain shall be one flesh,'" I muttered.

"Yes," he said, "I think the explanation must be something of that sort. There's more than that in it, though; these arms are other than flesh."

He sat silent for a time with his head bowed on his chest. Then he spoke again:

"I got sick of being alone at last, and was coming back when I met you at Fourteen Streams. I don't know what I shall do when I

21

do get home. I can never rest. I have—what do they call it—*Wanderlust*?"

"Does she ever speak to you from that other world?" I asked him. He shook his head sadly.

"No, never. But I know she lives somewhere beyond this world of ours. She must, because these arms live. So I try always to act as if she watches everything. I always try to do the right thing, but, anyway, these arms and hands would do good of their own accord. Just now up on the deck I was very frightened. I'd have saved myself at any cost almost, and let you go. But I could not do that. The hands clutched you. It is her will, so much stronger and purer than mine, that still persists. It is only when she does not exert it that I control these arms."

That was how I learnt the strangest tale that ever a man was told, and knew the miracle to which I owed my life.

It may be that Bob Masters was a coward. He always said that he was. Personally I do not believe it, for he had the sweetest nature I ever met.

He had nowhere to go to in England and seemed to have no friends. So I made him come down with me to Englehart, that dear old country seat of my family in the Western shires which was now mine.

Nancy lived in that country, too.

There was no reason why we should not get married at once. We had waited long enough.

I can see again the old, ivy-grown church where Nancy and I were wed, and Bob Masters standing by my side as best man.

I remember feeling in his pocket for the ring, and as I did so, I felt a hand grasp mine for a moment.

Then there was the reception afterwards, and speech-making—the usual sort of thing.

Later Nancy and I drove off to the station.

We had not said good-bye to Bob, for he'd insisted on driving to the station with the luggage; said he was going to see the last of us there.

He was waiting for us in the yard when we reached it, and walked with us on to the platform.

We stood there chatting about one thing and another, when I noticed that Nancy was not talking much and seemed rather pale. I was just going to remark on it when we heard the whistle of the train. There is a sharp curve in the permanent way outside the station, so that a train is on you all of a sudden.

Suddenly to my horror I saw Nancy sway backwards towards the edge of the platform. I tried vainly to catch her as she reeled and fell—right in front of the oncoming train. I sprang forward to leap after her, but hands grasped me and flung me back so violently that I fell down on the platform.

It was Bob Masters who took the place that should have been mine, and leapt upon the metals.

I could not see what happened then. The station-master says he saw Nancy lifted from before the engine when it was right upon her. He says it was as if she was lifted by the wind. She was quite close to Masters. "Near enough for him to have lifted her, sir, if he'd had arms." The two of them staggered for a moment, and together fell clear of the train.

Nancy was little the worse for the awful accident, bruised, of course, but poor Masters was unconscious.

We carried him into the waiting-room, laid him on the cushions there, and sent hot-foot for the doctor.

He was a good country practitioner, and, I suppose, knew the ordinary routine of his work quite well. He fussed about, hummed and hawed a lot.

"Yes, yes," he said, as if he were trying to persuade himself. "Shock, you know. He'll be better presently. Lucky, though, that he had no arms."

I noticed then, for the first time, that the sleeves of the coat had been shorn away.

"Doctor," I said, "how is he? Surely, if he isn't hurt he would not look like that. What exactly do you mean by shock?"

"Hum—er," he hesitated, and applied his stethoscope to Masters' heart again.

"The heart is very weak," he said at length. "Very weak. He's always very anæmic, I suppose?"

23

"No," I answered. "He's anything but that. He's——Good Lord, he's bleeding to death! Put ligatures on his arms. Put ligatures on his arms."

"Please keep quiet, Mr. Riverston," the doctor said. "It must have been a dreadful experience for you, and you are naturally very upset."

I raved and cursed at him. I think I should have struck him, but the others held me. They said they would take me away if I did not keep quiet.

Bob Masters opened his eyes presently, and saw them holding me.

"Please let him go," he said. "It's all right, old man. It's no use your arguing with them, they would not understand. I could never explain to them now, and they would never believe you. Besides, it's all for the best. Yes, the train went over them and I'm armless for the second time. But—not for long!"

I knelt by his side and sobbed. It all seemed so dreadful, and yet, I don't think that then I would have tried to stay his passing. I knew it was best for him.

He looked at me very affectionately.

"I'm so sorry that this should happen on your wedding-day," he said. "But it would have been so much worse for you if *she* had not helped."

His voice grew fainter and died away.

There was a pause for a time, and his breath came in great sighing sobs.

Then suddenly he raised himself on the cushions until he stood upright on his feet, and a smile broke over his face—a smile so sweet that I think the angels in Paradise must look like that.

His voice came strong and loud from his lips.

"Darling!" he cried. "Darling, your arms are round me once again! I come! I come!"

"One of the most extraordinary cases I have ever met with," the doctor told the coroner at the inquest. "He seemed to have all the symptoms of excessive hæmorrhage."

THE TOMTOM CLUE
SCUDAMORE JARVIS AND CECIL MORGAN

I HAD JUST SETTLED DOWN for a comfortable evening over the fire in a saddle-bag chair drawn up as close to the hearth as the fender would allow, with a plentiful supply of literature and whisky, and pipe and tobacco, when the telephone bell rang loudly and insistently. With a sigh I rose and took up the receiver.

"That you?" said a voice I recognised as that of Jack Bridges. "Can I come round and see you at once? It's most important. No, I can't tell you now. I'll be with you in a few minutes."

I hung the receiver up again, wondering what business could fetch Jack Bridges round at that time of the evening to see me. We had been the greatest of pals at school and at the 'Varsity, and had kept the friendship up ever since, despite my intermittent wanderings over the face of the globe. But during the last few days or so Jack had become engaged to Miss Glanville, the daughter of old Glanville, of South African fame, and as a love-sick swain I naturally expected to see very little of him, until after the wedding at any rate.

At this time of the evening, according to my ideas of engaged couples, he should be sitting in the stalls at some theatre, and not running round to see bachelor friends with cynical views on matrimony.

I had not arrived at a satisfactory solution when the door opened and Jack walked in. One glance at his face told me that he was in trouble, and without a word I pushed him into my chair and handed him a drink. Then I sat down on the opposite side of the

25

fire and waited for him to begin, for a man in need of sympathy does not want to be worried by questions.

He gulped down half his whisky and sat for a moment gazing into the fire.

"Jim, old man," he said at length, "I've had awful news."

"Not connected with Miss Glanville?" I asked.

"In a way, yes. It's broken off, but there's worse than that—far worse. I can hardly realise it; I feel numbed at present; it's too horrible. You remember that when you and I were at Winchester together my father was killed during the Matabele War?"

I nodded.

"Well," continued Jack, "I heard to-day that he was not killed by the Matabele, but was hanged in Bulawayo for murder. In other words, I am the son of a murderer."

"Hanged for murder!" I exclaimed in horror. "Surely there's some mistake?"

"No," groaned Jack, "it's true enough. I've seen the newspaper cutting of the time, and I'm the son of a murderer, who was also a forger, a thief, and a card-sharper. Old Glanville told me this evening. It was then that our engagement was broken off."

"Your mother?" I asked. "Have you seen her?"

Jack nodded.

"Poor little woman!" he groaned. "She has known all along, and her one aim and object in life has been to keep the awful truth from me. That was why I was told he died an honourable death during the war. I've often wondered why the little mother was always so sad, and so weighed down by trouble. Now I know. Good God, what her life must have been!"

He rose from his chair and paced up and down the room for a minute; then he stopped and stood in front of me, his face working with emotion.

"But I don't believe it, Jim," he said, and there was a ring in his voice. "I don't believe it, and neither does the little mother. It's impossible to reconcile the big, bluff man with the heart of a child, that I remember as my father, with murder, forgery, or any other crime. And yet, according to Glanville and the old newspapers he

26

showed me, Richard Bridges was one of the most unscrupulous ruffians in South Africa. In my heart of hearts I know he didn't do it, and though on the face of it there's no doubt, I'm going to try and clear his name. I am sailing for South Africa on Friday."

"Sailing for South Africa!" I exclaimed. "What about your work?"

"My work can go hang!" replied Jack heatedly. "I want to wipe away the stain from my father's name, and I mean to do it somehow. That's why I've run round to see you, old pal, for I want you to come with me. Knowing Rhodesia as you do, you're just the man to help me. Say you'll come?" he pleaded.

It seemed quite the forlornest hope I had ever heard of, but Jack's distress was so acute that I hadn't the heart to refuse.

"All right, Jack," I said, "I'm with you. But don't foster any vain hopes. Remember, it's twenty years ago. It will be a pretty tough job to prove anything after all these years."

During the voyage out we had ample time to go through the small amount of information about the long-forgotten case that Jack had been able to collect from the family solicitors.

In the year 1893, Richard Bridges, who was a mining engineer of some standing, had made a trip to Rhodesia with a view to gold and diamond prospecting. He had been accompanied by a friend, Thomas Symes, who, so far as we could ascertain, was an ex-naval officer; and the two, after a short stay at Bulawayo, had gone northward across the Guai river into what was in those days a practically unknown land. In a little over a year's time Bridges had returned alone—his companion having been, so he stated, killed by the Matabele, and for six months or so he led a dissolute life in Bulawayo and the district, which ended ultimately in his execution for murder. There was no doubt whatever about the murder, or the various thefts and forgeries that he was accused of, as he had made a confession at his trial, and we seemed to be on a wild-goose chase of the worst variety so far as I could see; but Jack, confident of his father's innocence, would not hear of failure.

"It's impossible to make surmises at this stage," he said. "On the face of it there appears to be little room for doubt, but no one who knew my father could possibly connect him with any sort of crime. Somehow or other, Jim, I've got to clear his name."

My memory went back to a tall, sunburnt man with a kindly manner who had come down to the school one day and put up a glorious feed at the tuck shop to Jack and his friends. Afterwards, at his son's urgent request, he had bared his chest to show us his tattooing of which Jack had, boy-like, often boasted to us. I recalled how we had gazed admiringly at the skilfully worked picture of Nelson with his empty sleeve and closed eye and the inscription underneath: "England expects that every man this day will do his duty." Jack had explained with considerable pride that this did not constitute all, as on his father's back was a wonderful representation of the *Victory*, and on other parts of his body a lion, a snake, and other *fauna*, but Richard Bridges had protested laughingly and refused to undress further for our delectation.

We reached Bulawayo, but no one in the city appeared to recall the case at all; indeed, Bulawayo had grown out of all recognition since Richard Bridges had passed through it on his prospecting trip. It was difficult to know where to start. Even the police could not help, and had no knowledge of where the murderer had been buried. No one but an old saloon-keeper and a couple of miners could recollect the execution even, and they, so far as they could remember, had never met Richard Bridges in the flesh, though his unsavoury reputation was well known to them.

In despair, Jack suggested a trek up country towards Barotseland, which was the district that Bridges and Symes had proposed to prospect, though, according to all accounts, Symes had been murdered by the Matabele before they reached the Guai river.

For the next month we trekked steadily northwards, having very fair sport; but, as I expected, extracting no information whatever from the natives about the two prospectors who had passed that way years before. At length, Jack became more or less reconciled to failure, and realising the futility of further search suggested a return to Bulawayo. As our donkey caravan was beginning to suffer severely from the fly, I concurred, and we started to travel slowly back to Bulawayo, shooting by the way.

One night after a particularly hard trek we inspanned at an old *kraal*, the painted walls of which told that at one time it had served as a royal residence, and as I had shot an eland cow that afternoon, which provided far more meat than we could consume, we invited the induna and his tribe to the feast. Not to be outdone in hospitality, the old chief produced the kaffir beer of the country, a liquid which has nothing to recommend it beyond the fact that it intoxicates rapidly.

A meat feast and a beer drink is a great event in the average kaffir's life, and as the evening wore on a general jollification started to the thump of tomtoms and the squeak of kaffir fiddles. There was one very drunk old Barotse, who sat close to me, and, accompanying himself with thumps on his tomtom, sang in one droning key a song about a man who kept snakes and lions inside him, and from whose chest the evil eye looked out. At least, so far as I could gather that was roughly the gist of the song; but as his tomtom was particularly large and most obnoxious I politely took it away from him, and Jack and I used it as a table for our gourds of kaffir beer, which we were pretending to consume in large quantities.

A gourd, however, is a top-heavy sort of drinking vessel, and in a very short time I had succeeded in spilling half a pint or so of my drink on the parchment of the drum. Not wishing to spoil the old gentleman's plaything, which he evidently valued above all things, I mopped up the beer with my handkerchief, and in doing so removed from the parchment a portion of the accumulated filth of ages.

"Hullo!" said Jack, taking the instrument from me and holding it up to the firelight. "There's a picture of some sort here. It looks like a man in a cocked hat."

He rubbed it hard with his pocket handkerchief, and the polishing brought more of the picture to light, till, plain enough in places and faded in others, there stood out, the portrait of a man in an old-fashioned naval uniform with stars on his breast, and underneath some letters in the form of a scroll.

"That's not native work," I exclaimed. "These are English letters," for I could distinctly make out the word "man" followed by a "t" and an "h." "Rub it hard, Jack."

The grease on the parchment refused to give way to further polishing, however, and remembering a bottle of ammonia I kept for insect bites, I mixed some with kaffir beer and poured it on the head of the tomtom. One touch of the handkerchief was sufficient once the strong alkali got to work, and out came the grand old face of Nelson and underneath his motto:

"England expects that every man this day will do his duty."

Jack dropped the drum as if it had bitten him.

"What does it mean?" he gasped. "My father had this on his chest. I remember it well!"

I was, however, too busy with the reverse end of the drum to heed him. On the other side the ammonia brought out a picture of the *Victory*, with the head of a roaring lion below it.

"Good God!" exclaimed Jack. "My father had that on his back. Quick, Jim, rub hard! There should be the family crest to the right—an eagle with a snake in its talons and R. B. underneath."

I rubbed in the spot indicated, and out came the crest and initials exactly as Jack had described them. There was something horribly uncanny and gruesome in finding the tattoo marks of the dead man on the parchment of a Barotse tomtom two hundred miles north of the Zambesi, and for a moment I was too overcome with astonishment to grasp exactly what it meant. Then it came to my mind in a flash that the parchment was nothing else than human skin, and Richard Bridges' skin at that. I put it down with sudden reverence, and, beckoning to its owner, demanded its full history. At first he showed signs of fear, but promising him a waist length of cloth if he told the truth, he squatted on his hams before us and began.

"Many, many moons ago, before the white men came to trade across the Big Water as they do now, two white baases came into this country to look for white stones and gold. One baas was bigger than the other, and on his chest and on his body were pictures of birds, and beasts, and strange things. On his chest was a great inkoos with one eye covered, and on his back a hut with trees growing straight up into the air from it. On his loins was a lion of great fierceness, and coiled round his waist was a hissing mamba (snake).

We were sore afraid, for the white baas told us he was bewitched, and that if harm came to either he would uncover the closed eye of the great inkoos upon his chest, which was the Evil Eye, and command him to blast the Barotse and their land for ever.

"So the white men were suffered to come and go in peace, for we dreaded the Evil Eye of the great inkoos. They toiled, these white baases, digging in the hillside and searching the riverbed; and then one day it came to pass that they quarrelled and fought, and the baas with the pictures was slain. We knew then that his medicine was bad medicine, otherwise the white baas without the pictures could not have killed him. So we were wroth and made to slay the other baas, but he shot us down with a fire stick and returned to his own country in haste. Then did I take the skin from the dead baas, for I loved him for his pictures, and I made them into a tomtom. I have spoken."

"Good heavens!" exclaimed Jack when I had translated the story. "Then my father was killed here in Barotseland, and it was Symes, his murderer, who went back to Bulawayo. It was that fiend Symes, also, who took my father's name, probably to draw any money that might have been left behind, and who, as Richard Bridges, was hanged for murder. Poor old dad," he added brokenly, "murdered, and his body mutilated by savages! But how glad I am to know that he died an honest man!"

With the evidence at hand it was easy to prove the identity of the murderer of twenty years ago, and, having settled the matter satisfactorily and cleared the dead man's name, Jack and I returned to England, where a few weeks later I had to purchase wedding garments in order that I might play the part of best man at Jack's wedding.

31

THE CASE OF SIR ALISTER MOERAN
MARGARET STRICKLAND

"ETHNE?" MY AUNT LOOKED AT ME with raised brows and smiled. "My dear Maurice, hadn't you heard? Ethne went abroad directly after Christmas, with the Wilmotts, for a trip to Egypt. She's having a glorious time!"

I am afraid I looked as blank as I felt. I had only landed in England three days ago, after two years' service in India, and the one thing I had been looking forward to was seeing my cousin Ethne again.

"Then, since you did not know she was away, you, of course, have not heard the other news?" went on my aunt.

"No," I answered in a wooden voice. "I've heard nothing."

She beamed. "The dear child is engaged to a Sir Alister Moeran, whom she met in Luxor. Everyone is delighted, as it is a splendid match for her. Lady Wilmott speaks most highly of him, a man of excellent family and position, and perfectly charming to boot."

I believe I murmured something suitable, but it was absurd to pretend to be overjoyed at the news. The galling part of it was that Aunt Linda knew, and was chuckling, so to speak, over my discomfiture.

"If you are going up to Wimberley Park," she went on sweetly, "you will probably meet them both, as your Uncle Bob has asked us all there for the February house-party. He cabled an invitation to Sir Alister as soon as he heard of the engagement. Wasn't it good of him?"

I replied that it was; then, having heard quite enough for one day of the charms of Ethne's *fiancé*, I took my leave.

That night, after cursing myself for a churl, I wrote and wished her good luck. The next morning I received a letter from Uncle Bob asking me to go to Wimberley; and early in the following week I travelled up to Cumberland. I received a warm welcome from the old General. As a boy I used to spend the greater part of my holidays with him, and being childless himself, he regarded me more or less as a son.

On February 16th Ethne, her mother, and Sir Alister Moeran arrived. I motored to the station to meet them. The evening was cold and raw and so dark that it was almost impossible to distinguish people on the badly lighted little platform. However, as I groped my way along, I recognised Ethne's voice, and thus directed, hurried towards the group. As I did so two gleaming, golden eyes flashed out at me through the darkness.

"Hullo!" I thought. "So she's carted along the faithful Pincher!" But the next moment I found I was mistaken, for Ethne was holding out both hands to me in greeting. There was no dog with her, and in the bustle that followed, I forgot to seek further for the solution of those two fiery lights.

"It was good of you to come, Maurice," Ethne said with unmistakable pleasure, then, turning to the man at her side, "Alister, this is my cousin, Captain Kilvert, of whom you have heard me speak."

We murmured the usual formalities in the usual manner, but as my fingers touched his, I experienced the most curious sensation down the region of my spine. It took me back to Burma and a certain very uncomfortable night that I once passed in the jungle. But the impression was so fleeting as to be indefinable, and soon I was busy getting everyone settled in the car.

So far, except that he possessed an exceptionally charming voice, I had no chance of forming an opinion of my cousin's *fiancé*. It was half-past seven when we got back to the house, so we all went straight up to our rooms to dress for dinner.

Everyone was assembled in the drawing-room when Sir Alister Moeran came in, and I shall never forget the effect his appearance made. Conversation ceased entirely for an instant. There was a kind of breathless pause, which was almost audible as my uncle rose to greet him. In all my life I had never seen a handsomer man, and I don't suppose anyone else there had either. It was the most startling, arresting style of beauty one could possibly imagine, and yet, even as I stared at him in admiration, the word "Black!" flashed into my mind.

Black! I pulled myself up sharply. We English, who have lived out in the East, are far too prone to stigmatise thus anyone who shows the smallest trace of being a "half breed"; but in Sir Alister's case there was not even a suspicion of this. He was no darker than scores of men of my own nationality, and besides, he belonged, I knew, to a very old Scottish family. Yet, try as I would to strangle the idea, all through the evening the same horrible, unaccountable notion clung to me.

That he was the personality of the gathering there was not the slightest doubt. Men and women alike seemed attracted by him, for his individuality was on a par with his looks.

Several times during dinner I glanced at Ethne, but it was easy to see that all her attention was taken up by her lover. Yet, oddly enough, I was not jealous in the ordinary way. I saw the folly of imagining that I could stand a chance against a man like Moeran, and, moreover, he interested me too deeply. His knowledge of the East was extraordinary, and later, when the ladies had retired, he related many curious experiences.

"Might I ask," said my uncle's friend, Major Faucett, suddenly, "whether you were in the Service, or had you a Government appointment out there?"

Sir Alister smiled, and under his moustache I caught the gleam of strong, white teeth.

"As a matter of fact, neither. I am almost ashamed to say I have no profession, unless I may call myself an explorer."

"And why not?" put in Uncle Bob. "Provided your explorations were to some purpose and of benefit to the community in general, I consider you are doing something worth while."

"Exactly," Sir Alister replied. "From my earliest boyhood I have always had the strangest hankering for the East. I say strange, because to my parents it was inexplicable, neither of them having the slightest leaning in that direction, though to me it seemed the most natural desire in the world. I was like an alien in a foreign land, longing to get home. I recollect, as a child, my nurse thought me a beastly uncanny kid because I loved to lie in bed and listen to the cats howling and fighting outside. I used to put my head half under the blankets and imagine I was in my lair in the jungle, and those were the jackals and panthers prowling around outside."

"I suppose you'd been reading adventure books," Uncle Bob said, with a laugh. "I played at much the same game when I was a youngster, only in my case it was Redskins."

"Possibly," Sir Alister answered with a slight shrug, "only mine wasn't a game that I played with any other boys, it was a gnawing desire, which simply had to be satisfied; and the opportunity came. When I was fourteen, the father of a school friend of mine, who was going out to India, asked me to go out with him and the boy for the trip. Of course, I went."

"I wonder," the Major remarked, "that you ever came back once you got there, since you were so frightfully keen."

"I was certain I should return," he replied grimly.

A pause followed his last words, then Uncle Bob rose and led the way to the drawing-room, where for the remainder of the evening Sir Alister was chiefly monopolised by the ladies.

"WELL, MAURICE," Uncle Bob said, when on the following evening I was sitting in his study having my usual before-dinner chat with him, "and how do you like Ethne's future husband?"

I hesitated. "I—I really don't know," I replied.

"Come, boy," he said, with his whimsical smile, "why not be frank and own to a very natural jealousy?"

"Because," I answered simply, "the feeling Sir Alister Moeran inspires in me is not jealousy, curiously enough. It's something else, something indefinable that comes over me now and again. Dogs don't like him, and that's always a bad sign, to my thinking."

My uncle's bushy eyebrows went up slightly.

"When did you make this discovery?"

"This morning," I replied. "You know I took him and Ethne round the place. Well, the first thing I noticed was that Mike refused to come with us, although both Ethne and I called him. As we passed through the hall he slunk away into the library. I thought it a bit strange, as he's usually so frantic to go out with me. Still, I didn't attach any significance to the matter until later, when we visited the kennels. I don't know why, but one takes it for granted that a man is keen on dogs somehow and—"

"Isn't Sir Alister?"

"They are not keen on him, anyhow," I answered grimly. "They had heard my voice as we approached and were all barking with delight, but directly we entered the place there was a dead silence, save for a few ominous growls from Argo. It was a most extraordinary sight. They all bristled up, so to speak, sniffing the air though on the scent of something. I let Bess and Fritz loose, but instead of jumping up, as they usually do, they hung back and showed the whites of their eyes in a way I've never seen before. I actually had to whistle to them sharply several times before they came, and then it was in a slinking manner, taking good care to put Ethne and me between themselves and Moeran, and looking askance at him the whole while."

"H'm!" murmured the General with puckered brows. "That was certainly odd, very odd!"

"It was," I agreed, warming to the subject, "but there's odder still to come. I dare say you'll think it all my fancy, but the minute those animals put their heads up and sniffed in that peculiar way, I distinctly smelt the musky, savage odour of wild beasts. You know it well, anyone who has been through a jungle does."

Uncle Bob nodded. "I know it, too; 'Musky' is the very word—the smell of sun-warmed fur. Jove, how it carries me back! I remember once, years ago, coming upon a litter of lion cubs, in a cave, when I was out in Africa—"

"Yes! Yes!" I cried eagerly. "And that is what I smelt this morning. Those dogs smelt it, too. They felt that there was something alien, abnormal in their midst."

"That something being—Sir Alister Moeran?"

I felt myself flush up under his gaze. I got up and walked about the room.

36

"I don't understand it," I said doggedly. "I tell you plainly, Uncle Bob, I don't understand. My impression of the man last night was 'black,' but he's not black, I know that perfectly well, no more than you or I are, and yet I can't get over the behaviour of those hounds. It wasn't only one of 'em, it was the whole lot. They seemed to regard him as their natural enemy! And that smell! I'm sure Ethne detected it too, for she kept glancing about her in a startled, mystified way."

"And Sir Alister?" queried the General. "Do you mean to say he did not notice anything amiss?"

I shrugged my shoulders. "He didn't appear to. I called attention myself to the singular attitude of the hounds, and he said quite casually: 'Dogs never do take to me much.'"

Uncle Bob gave a short laugh. "Our friend is evidently not sensitive." He paused and rubbed his chin thoughtfully, then added: "It certainly is rather curious, but, for Heaven's sake, boy, don't get imagining all sorts of things!"

This nettled me and made me wish I had held my tongue. I was quite aware that my story might have sounded somewhat fantastic from a stranger; still, he ought to have known me better than to accuse me of imagination. I abruptly changed the subject, and shortly after left the room.

But I could not banish from my mind the incident of the morning. I could not forget the appealing faces of those dogs. Ethne and Sir Alister had left me there and returned to the house together, and, after their departure, those poor, dumb beasts had gathered round me in a way that was absolutely pathetic, licking and fondling my hands, as though apologising for their previous misconduct. Still, I understood. That bristling up their spines was precisely the same sensation I had experienced when I first met Sir Alister Moeran.

As I was slowly mounting the stairs on my way up to dress, I heard someone running up after me, and turned round to find Ethne beside me.

"Maurice," she said, rather breathlessly, "tell me, you did not punish Fritz and Bess for not coming at once when you called them this morning?"

"No," I answered.

She gave a nervous little laugh. "I'm glad of that. I thought per-haps—" She stopped short, then rushed on, "You know how queer mother is about cats—can't bear one in the room, and how they always fly out directly she comes in? Well, dogs are the same with Alister. He—he told me so himself. It seems funny to me, and I suppose to you, because we're so fond of all kinds of animals; but I don't really see why it should be any more extraordinary to have an antipathy for dogs than for cats, and no one thinks anything of it if you dislike cats."

"That is so," I said thoughtfully.

"Anyway," she went on, "it is not our own fault if a certain ani-mal does not instinctively take to us."

"Of course not," I replied stoutly. "You're surely not worrying about it, are you?"

She hastened to assure me that she was not, but I could see that my indorsing her opinion was a great relief to her. She had been afraid that I should think it unnatural. I did for that matter, but I could not, of course, tell her so.

That night Sir Alister and I sat up late talking after the other men had retired. We had got on the subject of India and had been comparing notes as to our different adventures. From this we went on to discussing perilous situations and escapes, and it was then that he narrated to me a very curious incident.

"It happened when I was only twenty-one," he said, "the year after my father died. I think I told you that as soon as ever I be-came my own master, I packed up and was off to the East. I had a friend with me, a boy who had been my best pal at school. They used to call us 'Black and White.' He was fair and girlish-looking, and his name was Buchanan. He was just as keen on India as I was, and purposed writing a book afterwards on our experiences.

"Our intention was to explore the wildest, most savage districts, and as a start we selected the province of Orissa. The forests there are wonderful, and it is there, if anywhere, that the almost extinct Indian lion is still to be found. We engaged two sturdy hillmen to accompany us and pushed our way downwards from Calcutta over mountains, rivers and through some of the densest jungles I've ever traversed. It was on the outskirts of one of the latter that the tragedy took place. We had pitched our tents one evening after a long, tiring day, and turned in early to sleep, Buchanan and I in one, and the two Bhils in the other."

Sir Alister paused for a few moments, toying with his cigar in an abstracted manner, then continued in the same clear, even voice:

"When I awoke next morning, I found my friend lying beside me dead, and blood all round us! His throat was torn open by the teeth of some wild beast, his breast was horribly mauled and lacerated, and his eyes were wide, staring open, and their expression was awful. He must have died a hideous death and known it!"

Again he stopped, but I made no comment, only waited with breathless interest till he went on.

"I called the two men. They came and looked, and for the first time I saw terror written on their faces. Their nostrils quivered as though scenting something; then 'Tiger!' they gasped simultaneously.

"One of them said he had heard a stifled scream in the night, but had thought it merely some animal in the jungle. The whole thing was a mystery. How I came to sleep undisturbed through it all, how I escaped the same fate, and why the tiger did not carry off his prey—"

"You are sure it was a tiger?" I put in.

"I think there was no doubt of it," Sir Alister replied. "The Bhils swore the teeth-marks were unmistakable, and not only that, but I saw another case seven years later. The body of a young woman was found in the compound outside my bungalow, done to death in precisely the same way. And several of the natives testified as to there being a tiger in that vicinity, for they had found three or four young goats destroyed in similar fashion."

"Who was the girl?" I asked.

Moeran slowly turned his lucent, amber eyes upon me as he answered. "She was a German, a sort of nursery governess at the English doctor's. He was naturally frightfully upset about it, and a regular panic sprang up in the neighbourhood. The natives got a superstitious scare—thought one of their gods was wroth about

39

something and demanded sacrifice; but the white people were simply out to kill the tiger."

"And did they?" I queried eagerly.

Sir Alister shook his head. "That I can't say, as I left the place very soon afterwards and went up to the mountains."

A long silence followed, during which I stared at him in mute fascination. Then an unaccountable impulse made me say abruptly: "Moeran, how old are you?"

His finely-marked eyebrows went up in surprise at the irrelevance of my question, but he smiled.

"Funny you should ask! It so happens that it's my birthday tomorrow. I shall be thirty-five."

"Thirty-five!" I repeated. Then with a shiver I rose from my seat. The room seemed to have turned suddenly cold.

"Come," I said, "let's go to bed."

NEXT NIGHT AT DINNER I proposed Sir Alister's health, and we all drank to him and his "bride-to-be." They had that day definitely settled the date of their marriage for two months ahead; Ethne was looking radiant and everyone seemed in the best of spirits.

We danced and romped and played rowdy games like a pack of children. Nothing was too silly for us to attempt. While a one-step was in full swing some would-be wag suddenly turned off all the lights. It was then that for a moment I caught sight of a pair of glowing, fiery eyes shining through the darkness. Instantly my thoughts flew back to that meeting at the station, when I had fancied that Ethne had her dog in her arms. A chill, sinister feeling crept over me, but I kept my gaze fixed steadily in the same direction. The next minute the lights went up, and I found myself staring straight at Sir Alister Moeran. His arm was round Ethne's waist and she was smiling up into his face. Almost immediately they took up the dance again, and I and my partner followed suit. But all my gaiety had departed. An indefinable oppression seized me and clung to me for the rest of the evening.

As I emerged from my room next morning I saw old Giles, the butler, hurrying down the corridor towards me.

40

"Oh, Mr. Maurice—Captain Kilvert, sir!" he burst out, consternation in every line of his usually stolid countenance. "A dreadful thing has happened! How it's come about I can't for the life of me say, and how we're going to tell the General, the Lord only knows!"

"What?" I asked, seizing him by the arm. "What is it?"

"The dawg, sir," he answered in a hoarse whisper, "Mike—in the study—"

I waited to hear no more, but strode off down the stairs, Giles hobbling beside me as fast as he could, and together we entered the study.

In the middle of the floor lay the body of Mike. A horrible foreboding gripped me, and I quickly knelt down and raised the dog's head. His neck was torn open, bitten right through to the windpipe, the blood still dripping from it into a dark pool on the carpet.

A cold, numbing sensation stole down my spine and made my legs grow suddenly weak. Beads of perspiration gathered on my forehead as I slowly rose to my feet and faced Giles.

"What's the meaning of it, sir?" he asked, passing his hand across his brow in utter bewilderment. "That dawg was as right as possible when I shut up last night, and he couldn't have got out."

"No," I answered mechanically, "he couldn't have got out."

"Looks like some wild beast had attacked him," muttered the old man, in awed tones, as he bent over the lifeless body. "D'ye see the teeth marks, sir? But it's not possible—not possible."

"No," I said again, in the same wooden fashion. "It's not possible."

"But how're we going to account for it to the General?" he cried brokenly. "Oh, Mr. Maurice, sir, it's dreadful!"

I nodded. "You're right, Giles! Still, it isn't your fault, nor mine. Leave the matter to me. I'll break it to my uncle."

It was a most unenviable task, but I did it. Poor Uncle Bob! I shall never forget his face when he saw the mutilated body of the dog that for years had been his faithful companion. He almost wept, only rage and resentment against the murderer were so strong in him that they thrust grief for the time into the background. The mysterious, incomprehensible manner of the dog's death only added to his anger, for there was apparently no one on whom to wreak his vengeance.

41

The news caused general concern throughout the house, and Ethne was frightfully upset.

"Oh, Alister, isn't it awful?" she exclaimed, tears standing in her pretty blue eyes. "Poor, darling Mike!"

"Yes," he answered rather absently. "It's most unfortunate. Valuable dog, too, wasn't it?"

I walked away. The man's calm, handsome face filled me suddenly with unspeakable revulsion. The atmosphere of the room seemed to become heavy and noisome. I felt compelled to get out into the open to breathe.

I found the General tramping up and down the drive in the rain, his chin sunk deep into the collar of his overcoat, his hat pulled low down over his eyes. I joined him without speaking, and in silence we paced side by side for another quarter of an hour.

"Uncle Bob," I said abruptly at last, "take my advice. Have one of the hounds indoors to-night—Princep, he's a good watch-dog."

The General stopped short in his walk and looked at me.

"You've something on your mind, boy. What is it?"

"This," I answered grimly. "Whoever, or whatever killed Mike was in the house last night, or got in, after Giles shut up. It may still be there for all we know. In the dark, dark deeds are done, and—well, I think it's wise to take precautions."

"Good God, Maurice, if there is any creature in hiding, we'll soon have it out! I'll have the place searched now. But the thing's impossible, absurd!"

I shrugged my shoulders. "Then Mike died a natural death?"

"Natural?" he echoed fiercely. "Don't talk rubbish!"

"In that case," I said quietly, "you'll agree to let one of the dogs sleep in."

He gave me a long, troubled, searching look, then said gruffly: "Very well, but don't make any fuss about it. Women are such nervous beings and we don't want to upset anyone."

"You needn't be afraid of that," I replied, "I'll manage it all right."

There was no further talk of Mike that day. The visitors, seeing how distressed the General was, by tacit consent avoided the subject, but everyone felt the dampening effect.

42

That night, before I retired to my room, I took a lantern, went out to the kennels and brought in Princep, a pure-bred Irish setter. He was a dog of exceptional intelligence, and when I spoke to him, explaining the reason of his presence indoors, he seemed to know instinctively what was required of him.

As I passed the study I noticed a light coming from under the door. Somewhat surprised, I turned the handle and looked in. My uncle was seated before his desk in the act of loading a revolver. He glanced up sharply as I entered.

"Oh, it's you, is it? Got the dog in?"

"Yes," I replied, "I've left him in the library with the door open."

He regarded the revolver pensively for a few moments, then laid it down in front of him.

"You've no theory as to this—this business?"

I shook my head, I could offer no explanation. Yet all the while there lurked, deep down in my heart, a hideous suspicion, a suspicion so monstrous that had I voiced it, I should probably have been considered mad. And so I held my peace on the subject and merely wished my uncle good-night.

It was about one o'clock when I got into bed, but my brain was far too agitated for sleep. Something I had heard years ago, some old wives' tales about a man's life changing every seven years, kept dinning in my head. I was striving to remember how the story went, when a slight sound outside caught my ear. In a second I was out of bed and had silently opened the door. As I did so, someone passed close by me down the corridor.

Cautiously, with beating heart, I crept out and followed. However, I almost exclaimed aloud in my amazement, for the light from a window fell full on the figure ahead of me, and I recognised my cousin Ethne. She was sleep-walking, a habit she had had from her childhood, and which apparently she had never outgrown.

For some minutes I stood there, undecided how to act, while she passed on down the stairs, out of sight. To wake her I knew would be wrong. I knew, also, that she had walked thus a score of times without coming to any harm. There was, therefore, no reason why I should not return to my room and leave her to her wandering, yet still I remained rooted to the spot, all my senses strained, alert. And then suddenly I heard Princep whine. A series of low, stertorous growls followed, growls that made my blood run cold! With swift, noiseless steps, I stole along to the minstrel's gallery which overlooked that portion of the hall that communicated with the library. As I did so, there arose from immediately below me a succession of sharp snarls, such as a dog gives when he is in deadly fear or pain.

A shaft of moonlight fell across the polished floor, and by its aid I was just able to distinguish the form of Princep crouched against the wainscoting. He was breathing heavily, his head turned all the while towards the opposite side of the room. I looked in the same direction. Out of the darkness gleamed two fiery, golden orbs, two eyes that moved slowly to and fro, backwards and forwards, as though the Thing were prowling round and round. Now it seemed to crouch as though ready to spring, and I could hear the savage growling as of some beast of prey.

As I watched, horrified, fascinated, a *portière* close by was lifted, and the white-robed figure of Ethne appeared. All heedless of danger she came on across the hall, and the Thing, with soft, stealthy tread, came after her. I knew then that there was not an instant to be lost, and like a flash I darted along the gallery and down the stairs. But ere I gained the hall a piercing scream rent the air, and I was just in time to see Ethne borne to the ground by a great, dark form, which had sprung at her like a tiger.

Half frantic, I dashed forward, snatching as I did so a rapier from the wall, the only weapon handy. But before I reached the spot, a voice from the study doorway called: "Stop!" and the next moment the report of a pistol rang out.

"Good God!" I cried. "Who have you shot?"

"Not the girl," answered the grim voice of my uncle, "you may trust my aim for that! I fired at the eyes of the Thing. Here, quick, get lights and let's see what has happened."

But my one and only thought was for Ethne. Moving across to the dark mass on the floor, I stretched out my hand. My fingers touched a smooth, fabric-like cloth, but the smell was the smell of fur, the musky, sun-warmed fur of the jungle! With sickening repugnance, I seized the Thing by its two broad shoulders and rolled it over. Then I carefully raised Ethne from the ground. At that moment Giles and a footman appeared with candles. In silence my uncle took one and came towards me, the servants with scared, blanched countenances following.

The light fell full upon the dead, upturned face of Sir Alister Moeran. His upper lip was drawn back, showing the strong, white teeth. The two front ones were tipped with blood. Instantly my eyes turned to Ethne's throat, and there I saw deep, horrible marks, like the marks of a tiger's fangs; but, thank God, they had not penetrated far enough to do any serious injury! My uncle's shot had come just in time to save her.

"Merely fainted, hasn't she?" he asked anxiously.

I nodded. My relief at finding this was so, was too great for words.

"Heaven be praised!" I heard him mutter. Then lifting my beautiful, unconscious burden in my arms, I carried her upstairs to her room.

CAN I EXPLAIN, can anyone explain, the mysterious vagaries of atavism? I only know that there are amongst us, rare instances fortunately, but existent nevertheless—men with the souls of beasts. They may be cognisant of the fact or otherwise. In the case of Sir Alister I feel sure it was the latter. He had probably no more idea than I what far-reaching, evil strain it was that came out in his blood and turned him, every seven years, practically into a vampire.

THE KISS
M. E. ROYCE

I

THE QUIET OF THE DESERTED BUILDING incircled the little, glowing room as the velvet incircles the jewel in its case. Occasionally faint sounds came from the distance—the movements of cleaners at work, a raised voice, the slamming of a door.

The man sat at his desk, as he had sat through the busy day, but he had turned sideways in his seat, the better to regard the other occupant of the room.

She was not beautiful—had no need to be. Her call to him had been the saner call of mind to mind. That he desired, besides, the passing benediction of her hands, the fragrance of her corn-gold hair, the sight of her slenderness: this she had guessed and gloried in. Till now, he had touched her physical self neither in word nor deed. To-night, she knew, the barriers would be down; to-night they would kiss.

Her quiet eyes, held by his during the spell that had bound them speechless, did not flinch at the breaking of it.

"The Lord made the world and then He made this rotten old office," the man said quietly. "Into it He put you—and me. What, before that day, has gone to the making and marring of me, and the making and perfecting of you, is not to the point. It is enough that we have realised, heart, and soul, and body, that you are mine and I am yours."

"Yes," she said.

He fell silent again, his eyes on her hungrily. She felt them and longed for his touch. But there came only his voice.

"I want you. The first moment I saw you I wanted you. I thought then that, whatever the cost, I would have you. That was in the early days of our talks here—before you made it so courageously clear to me that it would never be possible for you to ignore my marriage and come to me. That is still so, isn't it?"

She moved slightly, like a dreamer in pain, as again she faced the creed she had hated through many a sleepless night.

"It is so," she agreed. "And because it is so, you are going away to-morrow."

"Yes."

They looked at each other across the foot or two of intervening space. It was a look to bridge death with. But even beneath their suffering, her eyes voiced the tremulous waiting of her lips.

At last he found words.

"You are the most wonderful woman in the world—the pluckiest, the most completely understanding; you have the widest charity. I suppose I ought to thank you for it all; I can't—that's not my way. I have always demanded of you, demanded enormously, and received my measure pressed down and running over. Now I am going to ask this last thing of you: will you, of your goodness, go away—upstairs, anywhere—and come back in ten minutes' time? By then I shall have cleared out."

She looked at him almost incredulously, lips parted. Suddenly she seemed a child.

"You—I—" she stammered. Then rising to her feet, with a superb simplicity: "But, you must kiss me before you go. You must! You—simply *must*."

For the space of a flaming moment it seemed that in one stride he would have crossed to her side, caught and held her.

"For God's sake—!" he muttered, in almost ludicrous fear of himself. Then, with a big effort, he regained his self-control.

"Listen," he said hoarsely. "I want to kiss you so much that I daren't even get to my feet. Do you understand what that means? Think of it, just for a moment, and then realise that *I am not going to kiss you*. And I have kissed many women in my time, too, and shall kiss more, no doubt."

"But it's not because of that—?"

"That I'm holding back? No. Neither is it because I funk the torture of kissing you once and letting you go. It's because I'm afraid—for *you*."

"For me?"

"Listen. You have unfolded your beliefs to me and, though I don't hold them—don't attempt to live up to your lights—the realisation of them has given me a reverence for you that you don't dream of. I have put you in a shrine and knelt to you; every time you have sat in that chair and talked with me, I have worshipped you."

"It would not alter—all that," the girl said faintly, "if you kissed me."

"I don't believe that; neither do you—no, you don't! In your heart of hearts you admit that a woman like you is not kissed for the first and last time by a man like me. Suppose I kissed you now? I should awaken something in you as yet half asleep. You're young and pulsing with life, and there are—thank Heaven!—few layers of that damnable young-girl shyness over you. The world would call you primitive, I suppose."

"But I don't—"

"Oh, Lord, you must see it's all or nothing! You surely understand that after I had left you you would not go against your morality, perhaps, but you would adjust it, in spite of yourself, to meet your desires! I cannot—safely—kiss you."

"But you are going away for good!"

"For good! Child, do you think my going will be your safeguard? If you wanted me so much that you came to think it was right and good to want me, wouldn't you find me, send for me, call for me? And I should come. God! I can see the look in your eyes now, when the want had been satisfied, and you could not drug your creed any more."

Her breath came in a long sigh. Then she tried to speak; tried again.

"It is so, isn't it?" he asked.

She nodded. Speech was too difficult. With the movement a strand of the corn-gold hair came tumbling down the side of her face.

48

"Then, that being the case," said the man, with infinite gentleness, his eyes on the little, tumbling lock, "I shall not attempt so much as to touch your hand before you leave the room."

At the door she turned.

"Tell me once again," she said. "You *want* to kiss me?"

He gripped the arms of his chair; from where she stood, she could see the veins standing out on his hands.

"I want to kiss you," he said fiercely. "I want to kiss you. If there were any way of cutting off to-morrow—all the to-morrows—with the danger they hold for us—I would kiss you. I would kiss you, and kiss you, and kiss you!"

II

WHERE HER FEET took her during the thousand, thousand years that was his going she could never afterwards say; but she found herself at last at the top of the great building, at an open window, leaning out, with the rain beating into her eyes.

Far below her the lights wavered and later she remembered that echoes of a far-off tumult had reached her as she sat. But her ears held only the memory of a man's footsteps—the eager tread that had never lingered so much as a second's space on its way to her; that had often stumbled slightly on the threshold of her presence; that she had heard and welcomed in her dreams; that would not come again.

The raindrops lay like tears upon her face.

She brushed them aside, and, rising, put up her hands to feel the wet lying heavy on her hair. The coldness of her limbs surprised her faintly. Downstairs she went again, the echoes mocking every step.

She closed the door of the room behind her and idly cleared a scrap of paper from a chair. Mechanically her hands went to the litter on his desk and she had straightened it all before she realised that there was no longer any need. To-morrow would bring a voice she did not know; would usher a stranger into her room to take her measure from behind a barrier of formality. For the rest there would be work, and food, and sleep.

These things would make life—life that had been love.

She put on her hat and coat. The room seemed smaller some-how and shabbier. The shaded lights that had invited, now merely irritated; the whimsical disorder of books and papers spoke only of an uncompleted task. Gone was the glamour and the promise and the good comradeship. He had taken them all. She faced to-morrow, and to-morrow, and to-morrow empty-handed—in her heart the memory of words that had seared and healed in a breath, and the dead dream of a kiss. Her throat ached with the pain of it.

And then suddenly she heard him coming back!

She stiffened. For one instant, mind and body, she was rigid with the sheer wonder of it. Then, as the atmosphere of the room surged back, tense with vitality, her mind leapt forward in wel-come. He was coming back, coming back! The words hammered themselves out to the rhythm of the eager tread that never lingered so much as a second's space on its way to her, that stumbled slightly on the threshold of her presence.

By some queer, reflex twist of memory, her hands brushed imaginary raindrops from her face and strayed uncertainly to where the wet had lain on her hair.

The door opened and closed behind him.

"I've come back. I've come back to kiss you. Dear—*dear*!"

Her outflung hand checked him in his stride towards her. Words came stammering to her lips.

"Why—but—this isn't—I don't understand! All you said—it was true, surely? It was cruel of you to make me know it was true and then come back!"

"Let me kiss you—let me, let me!" He was overwhelming her, ignoring her resistance. "I must kiss you, I must kiss you." He said it again and again.

"No, no, you shan't—you can't play with me! You said you were afraid for me, and you made me afraid, too—of my weakness—of the danger—of my longing for you—"

"Let me kiss you! Yes, you shall let me; you *shall* let me." His arms held her, his face touched hers.

50

"Aren't you afraid any more? Has a miracle happened—may we kiss in spite of to-morrow?"

Inch by inch she was relaxing. All thought was slipping away into a great white light that held no to-morrows, nor any fear of them, nor of herself, nor of anything. The light crept to her feet, rose to her heart, her head. Through the radiance came his words.

"Yes, a miracle. Oh, my dear—my little child! I've come back to kiss you, little child."

"Kiss me, then," she said against his lips.

III

HAZILY SHE WAS AWARE that he had released her; that she had raised her head; that against the rough tweed of his shoulder there lay a long, corn-gold hair.

She laughed shakily and her hand went up to remove it; but he caught her fingers and held them to his face. And with the movement and his look there came over her in a wave the shame of her surrender, a shame that was yet a glory, a diadem of pride. She turned blindly away.

"Please," she heard herself saying, "let me go now. I want to be alone. I want to—please don't tell me to-night. To-morrow—"

She was at the door, groping for the handle. Behind her she heard his voice; it was very tender.

"I shall always kneel to you—in your shrine."

Then she was outside, and the chilly passages were cooling her burning face. She had left him in the room behind her; and she knew he would wait there long enough to allow her to leave the building. Almost immediately, it seemed, she was downstairs in the hall, had reached the entrance.

She confronted a group of white-faced, silent men.

"Why, is anything the matter? What has happened? O'Dell?"

The porter stood forward. He cleared his throat twice, but for all that, his words were barely audible.

"Yes, Miss Carryll. Good-night, miss. You'd best be going on, miss, if you'll excuse—"

51

Behind O'Dell stood a policeman; behind him again, a grave-eyed man stooped to an unusual task. It arrested her attention like the flash of red danger.

"Why is the door of your room being locked, O'Dell?" She knew her curiosity was indecent, but some powerful premonition was stirring in her, and she could not pass on. "Has there been an accident? Who is in there?"

Then, almost under her feet, she saw a dark pool lying sluggishly against the tiles; nearer the door another—on the pavement outside another—and yet another. She gasped, drew back, felt horribly sick; and, as she turned, she caught O'Dell's muttered aside to the policeman.

"Young lady's 'is seccereterry—must be the last that seen 'im alive. All told, 'tain't more'n 'arf-an-'our since 'e left. 'Good-night, O'Dell,' sez 'e. 'Miss Carryll's still working—don't lock 'er in,' sez 'e. Would 'ave 'is joke. Must 'ave gone round the corner an' slap inter the car. Wish to God the amberlance—"

Her cry cut into his words as she flung herself forward. Her fingers wrenched at the key of the locked door and turned it, in spite of the detaining hands that seemed light as leaves upon her shoulder, and as easily shaken off. Unhearing, unheeding, she forced her way into the glare of electric light flooding the little room—beating down on to the table and its sheeted burden. Before she reached it, knowledge had dropped upon her like a mantle.

Her face was grey as the one from which she drew the merciful coverings, but her eyes went fearlessly to that which she sought.

Against the rough tweed of the shoulder lay a long, corn-gold hair.

THE GOTH
ROY VICKERS

YOUNG CARGILL SMILED as Mrs. Lardner finished her account.

"And do you really think that the fact that the poor chap was drowned had anything to do with it?" he asked. "Why, you admit yourself that he was known to have been drinking just before he fell out of his boat!"

"You may say what you like," returned his hostess impressively, "but since first we came to live at Tryn yr Wylfa only four people besides poor Roberts have defied the Fates, and each of them was drowned within the year.

"They were all tourists," she added with something suspiciously like satisfaction.

"I am not a superstitious man myself," supplemented the Major. "But you can't get away from the facts, you know, Cargill."

Cargill said no more. He perceived that they had lived long enough in retirement in the little Welsh village to have acquired a pride in its legend.

The legend and the mountains are the two attractions of Tryn yr Wylfa—the official guidebook devotes an equal amount of space to each. It will tell you that the bay, across which the quarry's tramp steamers now sail, was once dry land on which stood a village. Deep in the water the remains of this village can still be seen in clear weather. But whosoever dares to look upon them will be drowned within the year. A local publication gives full details of those who have looked—and perished.

53

The legend had received an unexpected boom in the drowning of Roberts, which had just occurred. Roberts was a fisherman who had recently come from the South. One calm day in February he had rowed out into the bay in fulfilment of a drunken boast. He was drowned three days before Midsummer.

After dinner young Cargill forgot about it. He forgot almost everything except Betty Lardner. But, oddly enough, as he walked back to the hotel it was just Betty Lardner who made him think again of the legend. He was in love, and, being very young, wanted to do something insanely heroic. To defy the Fates by looking on the sunken village was an obvious outlet for heroism.

He must have thought a good deal about it before he fell asleep, for he remembered his resolution on the following morning.

After breakfast he sauntered along the brief strip of asphalt which the villagers believe to be a promenade. He was not actually thinking of the legend; to be precise, he was thinking of Betty Lardner, but he was suddenly reminded of it by a boatman pressing him for his custom.

"Yes," he said abruptly. "I will hire your boat if you will row me out to the sunken village. I want to look at it."

The Welshman eyed him suspiciously, perceived that he was not joking, and shook his head.

"Come," persisted Cargill, "I will make it a sovereign if you care to do it."

"Thank you, but indeed, no, sir," replied the Welshman. "Not if it wass a hundred sofereigns!"

"Surely you are not afraid?"

"It iss not fit," retorted the Welshman, turning on his heel.

It was probably this opposition that made young Cargill decide that it would be really worth while to defy the legend.

He did not approach the only other boatman. He considered the question of swimming. The knowledge that the distance there and back was nearly five miles did not render the feat impossible, for he was a champion swimmer.

But he soon thought of a better way. He went back to the hotel and sought out Bissett. Bissett was a fellow member of the Middle

54

Temple, as contentedly briefless as himself. And Bissett possessed a motor-boat.

Bissett was not exactly keen on the prospect.

"Don't you think it is rather a silly thing to do?" he reasoned. "Of course it's all rot in a way—it must be. But isn't it just as well to treat that sort of thing with respect?"

Eventually he agreed to take the motor-boat to within a few hundred yards of the spot. They would tow a dinghy, in which young Cargill could finish the journey.

It took young Cargill half-an-hour to find the spot. But he did find it, and he did look upon, and actually see, all that remained of the sunken village.

He felt vaguely ashamed of himself when he returned to dry land. He noticed that several of the villagers gave him unfriendly glances; and he resolved that he would say nothing of the matter to the Lardners.

They were having tea on the lawn when he dropped in. He thought that Mrs. Lardner's welcome was a trifle chilly. After tea Betty executed a quite deliberate manœuvre to avoid having him for a partner at tennis. But he ran her to earth later, when they were picking up the balls.

"How *could* you?" was all she said.

"I—I didn't know you knew," he stammered weakly.

"Of course everybody knows! It was all over the village before you returned.

"Can't you see what that legend meant to us?" she went on. "It was a thing of beauty. And now you have spoilt it. It's like burning down the trees of the Fairy Glen. You—you *Goth!*"

"But suppose I am drowned before the year is out—like Roberts?" he suggested jocularly.

"Then I will forgive you," she said. And to Cargill it sounded exactly as if she meant what she said.

A few days later he returned to town. For six months he thought little about the legend. Then he was reminded of it.

He had been spending a weekend at Brighton. On the return journey he had a first-class smoker in the rear of the train to himself. Towards the end of the hour he dozed and dreamt of the day he had looked on the sunken village. He was awakened when the train made its usual stop on the bridge outside Victoria.

It had been a pleasant dream, and he was still trying to preserve the illusion when his eye fell lazily on the window, and he noticed that there was a dense fog.

"Bit rough on the legend that I happened to be a Londoner!" he mused. "It isn't easy to drown a man in town!"

He stood up with the object of removing his dressing-case from the rack. But before he reached it there was the shriek of a whistle, a violent shock, and he was hurled heavily into the opposite seat.

It was not a collision in the newspaper sense of the word. No one was hurt. A local train, creeping along at four miles an hour, had simply missed its signal in the fog and bumped the Brighton train.

Young Cargill, in common with most other passengers put his head out of the window. He saw nothing—except the parapet of the bridge.

"By God!" he muttered. "If that other train had been going a little faster——"

He could just hear the river gurgling beneath him.

He had got over his fright by the time he reached Victoria.

"Just a common-place accident," he assured himself, as he drove in a taxi-cab to his chambers. "That's the worst of it! If I happened to be drowned in the ordinary way they'd swear it was the legend. I suppose, for that reason, I had better not take any risks. Anyhow, I needn't go near the sea until the year is out!"

The superstitious would doubtless affirm that the Fates had sent him one warning and, angered at his refusal to accept it, had determined to drive home the lesson of his own impotence. For when he arrived at his chambers he found a cablegram from Paris awaiting him.

"Hullo, this must be from Uncle Peter!" he exclaimed, as he tore open the envelope.

"*Fear uncle dying. Come at once.—Machell.*"

Machell was the elder Cargill's secretary, and young Cargill was the old man's heir.

It was not until he was in the boat-train that he realised that he was about to cross the sea.

It was a coincidence—an odd coincidence. When the ship tossed in an unusually rough crossing he was prepared to admit to himself that it was an uncanny coincidence.

He stayed a week in Paris for his uncle's funeral. When he made the return journey the Channel was like the proverbial mill pond. But it was not until the ship had actually put into Dover that he laughed at the failure of the Fates to take the opportunity to drown him.

He laughed, to be exact, as he was stepping down the gangway. At the end of the gangway the fold of the rug which he was carrying on his arm, caught in the railings. He turned sharply to free it and stepping back, cannoned into an officer of the dock. It threw him off his balance on the edge of the dockside.

Even if the official had not grabbed him, it is highly probable that he could have saved himself from falling into the water, because the gangway railing was in easy reach; and if you remember that he was a champion swimmer, you will agree that it is still more probable that he would not have been drowned, even if he had fallen.

But the incident made its impression. His thoughts reverted to it constantly during the next few days. Then he told himself that his attendance at the last rites of his uncle had made him morbid, and was more or less successful in dismissing the affair from his mind.

He had many friends in common with the Lardners. Early in February he was invited for a week's hunting to a house at which Betty Lardner was also a guest.

She had not forgotten. She did her best to avoid him, and succeeded remarkably well, in spite of the fact that their hostess, knowing something of young Cargill's feelings, made several efforts to throw them together.

One day at the end of the hunt he came alongside of her and they walked their horses home together. When he was sure that they were out of earshot he asked:

"You haven't forgiven me yet?"

"You know the conditions," she replied banteringly.

"You leave me no alternative to suicide," he protested.

"That would be cheating," she said. "You must be drowned honestly, or it's no good."

Then he made a foolish reply. He thought her humour forced and it annoyed him. Remember that he was exasperated. He had looked forward to meeting her, and now she was treating him with studied coldness over what still seemed to him a comparatively trifling matter.

"I am afraid," he said, "that that is hardly likely to occur. The fact of my being a townsman instead of a drunken boatman doesn't give your legend a fair chance!"

Less than an hour afterwards he was having his bath before dressing for dinner. The water was deliciously hot, and the room was full of steam. As he lay in the bath a drowsiness stole over him. Enjoying the keen physical pleasure of it, he thought what a wholly delightful thing was a hot bath after a day's hard hunting. His mind, bordering on sleep, dwelt lazily on hot baths in general. And then with a startling suddenness came the thought that, before now, men had been drowned in their baths!

With a shock he realised that he had almost fallen asleep. He tried to rouse himself, but a faintness had seized him. That steam—he could not breathe! He was certain he was going to faint.

With a desperate effort of the will he hurled himself out of the bath and threw open the window.

It must have been the bath episode that first aroused the sensation of positive fear in Cargill. For it was almost a month later when he surprised the secretary of that swimming club of which he was the main pillar by his refusal to take part in any events for the coming season.

He was beginning to take precautions.

Late one night, when taxi-cabs were scarce, he found that his quickest way to reach home would be by means of one of the tubes. He was in the descending lift when he suddenly remembered that that particular tube ran beneath the river. Suppose an accident should occur—a leakage! After all such a thing was within the bounds of possibility. Instantly there rose before him the vision of a black torrent roaring through the tunnel.

Without waiting for the lift to ascend he rushed to the staircase, and sweating with terror gained the street and bribed a loafer to find him a cab.

He made an effort to take himself seriously in hand after that. More than one acquaintance had lately told him that he was looking "nervy." In the last few weeks his sane and normal self seemed to have shrunk within him. But it was still capable of asserting itself under favourable conditions. It would talk aloud to the rest of him as if to a separate individual.

"Look here, old man, this superstitious nonsense is becoming an obsession to you," it said one fine April morning. "Yes, I mean what I say—an obsession! You must pull yourself together or you'll go stark mad, and then you'll probably go and throw yourself over the Embankment. That legend is all bosh! You're in the twentieth century, and you're not a drunken fisherman—"

"Hullo, young Cargill!"

The door burst open and Stranack, oozing health and sanity, glared at him.

"Jove! What a wreck you look!" continued Stranack. "You've been frousting too much. I'm glad I came. The car's outside, and we'll run down to Kingston, take a skiff and pull up to Molesey."

The river! Young Cargill felt the blood singing in his ears.

"I'm afraid I can't manage it. I—I've got an appointment this afternoon," he stammered.

Stranack perceived that he was lying, and wondered. For a few minutes he gossiped, while young Cargill was repeating to himself:

"You must pull yourself together. It's becoming an obsession. You must pull yourself together."

He was vaguely conscious that Stranack was about to depart. Stranack was already in the doorway. His chance of killing the obsession was slipping from him! A special effort and then:

"Stop!" cried Cargill. "I—I'll come with you, Stranack."

Oddly enough, he felt much better when they were actually on the river. He had never been afraid of water, as such. And the familiar scenery, together with the wholesome exercise of sculling, acted as a tonic to his nerves.

They pulled above Molesey lock. When they were returning, Stranack said:

"You'll take her through the lock, won't you?"

59

It was a needless remark, and if Stranack had not made it all might have been well. As a fact, it set Cargill asking himself why he should not take her through the lock. He was admitted to be a much better boatman than Stranack, and everyone knew that it required a certain amount of skill to manage a lock properly. Locks were dangerous if you played the fool. Before now people had been drowned in locks.

The rest was inevitable. He lost his head as the lower gates swung open, and broke the rule of the river by pushing out in front of a launch. The launch was already under way, and young Cargill trying to avoid it better, thrust with his boat-hook at the side of the lock. The thrust was nervous and ill-calculated, and the next instant the skiff had blundered under the bows of the launch.

It happened very quickly. The skiff was forced, broadside on, against the lock gates, and was splintered like firewood. Cargill fell backwards, struck his head heavily against the gates—and sank.

He returned to consciousness in the lock-keeper's lodge. He had been under water a dangerously long time before Stranack, who had suffered no more than a wetting, had found him. It had been touch and go for his life, but artificial respiration had succeeded.

He soon went to pieces after that.

From one of the windows of his chambers the river was just visible. One morning he deliberately pulled the blind down. The action was important. It signified that he had definitely given up pretending that he had the power of shaking off the obsession.

But if he could not shake it off, he could at least keep it temporarily at bay. He started a guerilla campaign against the obsession with the aid of the brandy bottle. He was rarely drunk, and as rarely sober.

He was sober the day he was compelled to call on an aunt who lived in the still prosperous outskirts of Paddington. It was one of his good days and, in spite of his sobriety, he had himself in very good control when he left his aunt.

In his search for a cab it became necessary for him to cross the canal. On the bridge he paused and, gripping the parapet, made a surprise attack upon his enemy.

Some children, playing on the tow path, helped him considerably. Their delightful sanity in the presence of the water was worth more to him than the brandy. He was positively winning the battle, when one of the children fell into the water.

For an instant he hesitated. Then, as on the night of the Tube episode, panic seized him. The next instant the man who was probably the best amateur swimmer in England, was running with all his might away from the canal.

When he reached his chambers he waited, with the assistance of the brandy, until his man brought him the last edition of the evening paper. A tiny paragraph on the back sheet told him of the tragedy.

An hour later his man found him face downwards on the hearthrug and, wrongly attributing his condition wholly to the brandy, put him to bed.

He was in bed about three weeks. The doctor, who was also a personal friend, was shrewd enough to suspect that the brandy was the effect, rather than the cause of the nerve trouble.

About the first week in June Cargill was allowed to get up.

"You've got to go away," said the doctor one morning. "You are probably aware that your nerves have gone to pieces. The sea is the place for you!"

The gasp that followed was scarcely audible, and the doctor missed it.

"You went to Tryn yr Wylfa about this time last year," continued the doctor. "Go there again! Go for long walks on the mountains, and put up at a temperance hotel."

He went to Tryn yr Wylfa.

The train journey of six hours knocked him up for another week. By the time he was strong enough for the promenade it was the fourteenth of June. He noticed the date on the hotel calendar, and realised that the Fates had another ten days in which to drown him.

He did not call on the Lardners. He felt that he couldn't—after the canal episode. Four of the ten days had passed before Betty Lardner ran across him on the promenade.

61

She noticed at once the change in him, and was kinder than she had ever been before.

"Next Saturday," he said, "is the anniversary!"

For answer she smiled at him, and he might have smiled back if he had not remembered the canal.

She met him each morning after that, so that she was with him on the day when he made his atonement.

There had been a violent storm in the early morning. It had driven one of the quarry steamers on to the long sand-bank that lies submerged between Tryn yr Wylfa and Puffin Island. The gale still lasted, and the steamer was in momentary danger of becoming a complete wreck.

There is no lifeboat service at Tryn yr Wylfa. It was impossible to launch an ordinary boat in such a sea.

Colonel Denbigh, the owner of the quarry and local magnate, who had been superintending what feeble efforts had been made to effect a rescue, answered gloomily when Betty Lardner asked him if there were any hope.

"It's a terrible thing," he jerked. "First time there has been a wreck hereabouts. It's hopeless trying to launch a boat—"

"Suppose a fellow were to swim out to the wreck with a life-line in tow?"

It was young Cargill who spoke.

The Colonel glared at him contemptuously.

"He would need to be a pretty fine swimmer," he returned.

"I don't want to blow my own trumpet, but I am considered to be one of the best amateur swimmers in the country," replied Cargill calmly. "If you will tell your men to get the line ready, I will borrow a bathing suit from somewhere."

They both stared at him in amazement.

"But you are still an invalid," cried Betty Lardner. "You—"

She stopped short and regarded him with fresh wonder. Somehow he no longer looked an invalid.

Mechanically she walked by his side to the little bathing office. Suddenly she clutched his arm.

"Jack," she said, "have you forgotten the—the legend?"

"Betty," he replied, "have you forgotten the crew?"

While he was undressing the attendant asked him some trivial question. He did not hear the man. His thoughts were far away. He was thinking of a group of children playing on the bank of a canal.

To the accompaniment of the Colonel's protests they fixed a belt on him, to which was attached the life-line.

He walked along the sloping wooden projection that is used as a landing stage for pleasure skiffs, walked until the water splashed over him. Then he dived into the boiling surf.

Thus it was that he earned Betty Lardner's forgiveness.

THE LAST ASCENT
E. R. PUNSHON

THE EXTRAORDINARY RAPIDITY with which a successful airman may achieve fame was well shown in the case of my friend, Radcliffe Thorpe. One week known merely to a few friends as a clever young engineer, the next his name was on the lips of the civilised world. His first success was followed by a series of remarkable feats, of which his flight above the Atlantic, his race with the torpedo-boat-destroyers across the North Sea, and his sensational display during the military manœuvres on Salisbury Plain, impressed his name and personality firmly upon the fickle mind of the public, and explains the tremendous excitement caused by his inexplicable disappearance during the great aviation meeting at Attercliffe, near London, towards the end of the summer.

Few people, I suppose, have forgotten the facts. For some time previously he had been devoting himself more especially to ascending to as great a height as possible. He held all the records for height, and it was known that at Attercliffe he meant to endeavour to eclipse his own achievements.

It was a lovely day, not a breath of wind stirring, not a cloud in the sky. We saw him start. We saw him fly up and up in great sweeping spirals. We saw him climb higher and ever higher into the azure space. We watched him, those of us whose eyes could bear the strain, as he dwindled to a dot and a speck, till at last he passed beyond sight.

It was a stirring thing to see a man thus storm, as it were, the walls of Heaven and probe the very mysteries of space. I remember

I felt quite annoyed with someone who was taking a cinematograph record. It seemed such a sordid, business-like thing to be doing at such a moment.

Presently the aeroplane came into sight again and was greeted with a sudden roar of cheering.

"He is doing a glide down," someone cried excitedly, and though someone else declared that a glide from such a height was unthinkable and impossible, yet it was soon plain that the first speaker was right.

Down through unimaginable thousands of feet, straight and swift swept the machine, making such a sweep as the eagle in its pride would never have dared. People held their breath to watch, expecting every moment some catastrophe. But the machine kept on an even keel, and in a few moments I joined with the others in a wild rush to the field at a little distance where the machine, like a mighty bird, had alighted easily and safely.

But when we reached it we doubted our own eyes, our own sanity. There was no sign anywhere of Radcliffe Thorpe!

No one knew what to say; we looked blankly at our neighbours, and one man got down on his hands and knees and peered under the body of the machine as if he suspected Radcliffe of hiding there. Then the chairman of the meeting, Lord Fallowfield, made a curious discovery.

"Look," he said in a high, shaken voice, "the steering wheel is jammed!"

It was true. The steering wheel had been carefully fastened in one position, and the lever controlling the planes had also been fixed so as to hold them at the right angle for a downward glide. That was strange enough, but in face of the mystery of Radcliffe's disappearance little attention was paid it.

Where, then, was its pilot? That was the question that was filling everybody's mind. He had vanished as utterly as vanishes the mist one sees rising in the sunshine.

It was supposed he must have fallen from his seat, but as to how that had happened, how it was that no fragment of his body or his clothing was ever found, above all, how it was that his aeroplane had returned, the engine cut off, the planes secured in correct position, no even moderately plausible explanation was ever put forward.

The loss to aeronautics was felt to be severe. From childhood Radcliffe had shown that, in addition to this, he had a marked aptitude for drawing, usually held at the service of his profession, but now and again exercised in producing sketches of his friends.

Among those who knew him privately he was fairly popular, though not, perhaps, so much so as he deserved; certainly he had a way of talking "shop" which was a trifle tiring to those who did not figure the world as one vast engineering problem, while with women he was apt to be brusque and short-mannered.

My surprise, then, can be imagined when, calling one afternoon on him and having to wait a little, I had noticed lying on his desk a crayon sketch of a woman's face. It was a very lovely face, the features almost perfect, and yet there was about it something unearthly and spectral that was curiously disturbing.

"Smitten at last?" I asked jestingly, and yet aware of a certain odd discomfort.

When, he saw what I was looking at he went very pale.

"Who is it?" I asked.

"Oh, just—someone!" he answered.

He took the sketch from me, looked at it, frowned and locked it away. As he seemed unwilling to pursue the subject, I went on to talk of the business I had come about, and I congratulated him on his flight of the day before in which he had broken the record for height. As I was going he said:

"By the way, that sketch—what did you think of it?"

"Why, that you had better be careful," I answered, laughing; "or you'll be falling from your high estate of bachelordom."

He gave so violent a start, his face expressed so much of apprehension and dismay, that I stared at him blankly. Recovering himself with an effort, he stammered out:

"It's not—I mean—it's an imaginary portrait."

"Then," I said, amazed in my turn, "you've a jolly sight more imagination than anyone ever credited you with."

The incident remained in my mind. As a matter of fact, practical Radcliffe Thorpe, absorbed in questions of strain and ease, his head full of cylinders and wheels and ratchets and the Lord knows what else, would have seemed to me the last man on earth to create that haunting, strange, unearthly face, human in form, but not in expression.

It was about this time that Radcliffe began to give so much attention to the making of very high flights. His favourite time was in the early morning, as soon as it was light. Then in the chill dawn he would rise and soar and wing his flight high and ever higher, up and up, till the eye could no longer follow his ascent.

I remember he made one of these strange, solitary flights when I was spending the week-end with him at his cottage near the Attercliffe Aviation Grounds.

I had come down from town somewhat late the night before, and I remember that just before we went to bed we went out for a few minutes to enjoy the beauty of a perfect night. The moon was shining in a clear sky, not a sound or a breath disturbed the sublime quietude; in the south one wondrous star gleamed low on the horizon. Neither of us spoke; it was enough to drink in the beauty of such rare perfection, and I noticed how Radcliffe kept his eyes fixed upwards on the dark blue vault of space.

"Are you longing to be up there?" I asked him jestingly.

He started and flushed, and he then went very pale, and to my surprise I saw that he was shivering.

"You are getting cold," I said. "We had better go in."

He nodded without answering, and, as we turned to go in, I heard quite plainly and distinctly a low, strange laugh, a laugh full of a honeyed sweetness that yet thrilled me with great fear.

"What's that?" I said, stopping short.

"What?" Radcliffe asked.

"Someone laughed," I said, and I stared all round and then upwards. "I thought it came from up there," I said in a bewildered way, pointing upwards.

He gave me an odd look and, without answering, went into the cottage. He had said nothing of having planned any flight for the next morning; but in the early morning, the chill and grey dawn, I was roused by the drumming of his engine. At once I jumped up out of bed and ran to the window.

The machine was raising itself lightly and easily from the ground. I watched him wing his god-like way up through the still, soft air till he was lost to view. Then, after a time, I saw him emerge again from those immensities of space. He came down in one long majestic sweep, and alighted in a field a little way away from the house, leaving the aeroplane for his mechanics to fetch up presently.

"Hullo!" I greeted him. "Why didn't you tell me you were going up?"

As I spoke I heard plainly and distinctly, as plainly as ever I heard anything in my life, that low, strange laugh, that I had heard before, so silvery sweet and yet somehow so horrible.

"What's that?" I said, stopping short and staring blankly upwards, for, absurd though it seems, that weird sound seemed to come floating down from an infinite height above us.

"Not high enough," he muttered like a man in an ecstasy. "Not high enough yet."

He walked away from me then without another word. When I entered the cottage he was seated at the table sketching a woman's face—the same face I had seen in that other sketch of his, spectral, unreal, and lovely.

"What on earth—?" I began.

"Nothing on earth," he answered in a strange voice. Then he laughed and jumped up, and tore his sketch across.

He seemed quite his old self again, chatty and pleasant, and with his old passion for talking "shop." He launched into a long explanation of some scheme he had in mind for securing automatic balancing.

I never told anyone about that strange, mocking laugh, in fact, I had almost forgotten the incident altogether when something brought every detail back to my memory. I had a letter from a person who signed himself "George Barnes."

Barnes, it seemed, was the operator who had taken the pictures of that last ascent, and as he understood I had been Mr. Thorpe's greatest friend, he wanted to see me. Certain expressions in the letter aroused my curiosity. I replied. He asked for an appointment at a time that was not very convenient, and finally I arranged to call at his house one evening.

It was one of those smart little six-room villas of which so many have been put up in the London suburbs of late. Barnes was buying it on the instalment system, and I quite won his heart by complimenting him on it. But for that, I doubt if anything would have come of my visit, for he was plainly nervous and ill at ease and very repentant of ever having said anything. But after my compliment to the house we got on better.

"It's on my mind," he said; "I shan't be easy till someone else knows."

We were in the front room where a good fire was burning—in my honour, I guessed, for the apartment had not the air of being much used. On the table were some photographs. Barnes showed them me. They were enlargements from those he had taken of poor Radcliffe's last ascent.

"They've been shown all over the world," he said. "Millions of people have seen them."

"Well?" I said.

"But there's one no one has seen—no one except me."

He produced another print and gave it to me. I glanced at it. It seemed much like the others, having been apparently one of the last of the series, taken when the aeroplane was at a great height. The only thing in which it differed from the others was that it seemed a trifle blurred.

"A poor one," I said; "it's misty."

"Look at the mist," he said.

I did so. Slowly, very slowly, I began to see that that misty appearance had a shape, a form. Even as I looked I saw the features of a human countenance—and yet not human either, so spectral was it, so unreal and strange. I felt the blood run cold in my veins and the hair bristle on the scalp of my head, for I recognised beyond all doubt that this face on the photograph was the same as that Radcliffe had sketched. The resemblance was absolute, no one who had seen the one could mistake the other.

"You see it?" Barnes muttered, and his face was almost as pale as mine.

"There's a woman," I stammered, "a woman floating in the air by his side. Her arms are held out to him."

"Yes," Barnes said. "Who was she?"

The print slipped from my hands and fluttered to the ground. Barnes picked it up and put it in the fire. Was it fancy or, as it flared up, and burnt and was consumed, did I really hear a faint laugh floating downwards from the upper air?

"I destroyed the negative," Barnes said, "and I told my boss something had gone wrong with it. No one has seen that photograph but you and me, and now no one ever will."

THE TERROR BY NIGHT
LEWIS LISTER

MAYNARD DISINCUMBERED HIMSELF from his fishing-creel, stabbed the butt of his rod into the turf, and settled down in the heather to fill a pipe. All round him stretched the undulating moor, purple in the late summer sunlight. To the southward, low down, a faint haze told where the sea lay. The stream at his feet sang its queer, crooning moor-song as it rambled onward, chuckling to meet a bed of pebbles somewhere out of sight, whispering mysteriously to the rushes that fringed its banks of peat, deepening to a sudden contralto as it poured over granite boulders into a scum-flecked pool below.

For a long time the man sat smoking. Occasionally he turned his head to watch with keen eyes the fretful movements of a fly hovering above the water. Then a sudden dimple in the smooth surface of the stream arrested his attention. A few concentric ripples widened, travelled towards him, and were absorbed in the current. His lips curved into a little smile and he reached for his rod. In the clear water he could see the origin of the ripples; a small trout, unconscious of his presence, was waiting in its hover for the next tit-bit to float downstream. Presently it rose again.

"The odds are ten to one in your favour," said the man. "Let's see!"

He dropped on one knee and the cast leapt out in feathery coils. Once, twice it swished; the third time it alighted like thistledown on the surface. There was a tiny splash, a laugh, and the little green-heart rod flicked a trout high over his head. It was the merest baby—half-an-ounce, perhaps—and it fell from the hook into the herbage some yards from the stream.

"Little ass!" said Maynard. "That was meant for your big brother."

He recovered his cast and began to look for his victim. Without avail he searched the heather, and as the fateful seconds sped, at last laid down his rod and dropped on hands and knees to probe among the grass-stems.

For a while he hunted in vain, then the sunlight showed a golden sheen among some stones. Maynard gave a grunt of relief, but as his hand closed round it a tiny flutter passed through the fingerling; it gave a final gasp and was still. Knitting his brows in almost comical vexation, he hastened to restore it to the stream, holding it by the tail and striving to impart a life-like wriggle to its limpness.

"Buck up, old thing!" he murmured encouragingly. "Oh, buck up! You're all right, really you are!"

But the "old thing" was all wrong. In fact, it was dead.

Standing in the wet shingle, Maynard regarded the speckled atom as it lay in the palm of his hand.

"A matter of seconds, my son. One instant in all eternity would have made just the difference between life and death to you. And the high gods denied it you!"

On the opposite side of the stream, set back about thirty paces from the brink, stood a granite boulder. It was as high as a man's chest, roughly cubical in shape; but the weather and clinging moss had rounded its edges, and in places segments had crumbled away, giving foothold to clumps of fern and starry moor-flowers. On three sides the surrounding ground rose steeply, forming an irregular horseshoe mound that opened to the west. Perhaps it was the queer amphitheatrical effect of this setting that connected up some whimsical train of thought in Maynard's brain.

"It would seem as if the gods had claimed you," he mused, still holding the corpse. "You shall be a sacrifice—a burnt sacrifice to the God of Waste Places."

He laughed at the conceit, half-ashamed of his own childishness, and crossing the stream by some boulders, he brushed away

72

the earth and weed from the top of the great stone. Then he re-traced his steps and gathered a handful of bleached twigs that the winter floods had left stranded along the margin of the stream. These he arranged methodically on the cleared space; on the top of the tiny pyre he placed the troutlet.

"There!" he said, and smiling gravely struck a match. A faint column of smoke curled up into the still air, and as he spoke the lower rim of the setting sun met the edge of the moor. The evening seemed suddenly to become incredibly still, even the voice of the stream ceasing to be a sound distinct. A wagtail bobbing in the shallows fled into the waste. Overhead the smoke trembled up-wards, a faint stain against a cloudless sky. The stillness seemed almost acute. It was as if the moor were waiting, and holding its breath while it waited. Then the twigs upon his altar crackled, and the pale flames blazed up. The man stepped back with artistic ap-preciation of the effect.

"To be really impressive, there ought to be more smoke," he continued.

Round the base of the stone were clumps of small flowers. They were crimson in colour and had thick, fleshy leaves. Hastily, he snatched a handful and piled it on the fire. The smoke darkened and rose in a thick column; there was a curious pungency in the air.

Far off the church-bell in some unseen hamlet struck the hour. The distant sound, coming from the world of men and every-day affairs, seemed to break the spell. An ousel fluttered across the stream and dabbled in a puddle among some stones. Rabbits be-gan to show themselves and frisk with lengthened shadows in the clear spaces. Maynard looked at his watch, half-mindful of a train to be caught somewhere miles away, and then, held by the peace of running water, stretched himself against the sloping ground.

The glowing world seemed peopled by tiny folk, living out their timid, inscrutable lives around him. A water-rat, passing bright-eyed upon his lawful occasion, paused on the border of the stream to consider the stranger, and was lost to view. A stagnant pool among some reeds caught the reflection of the sunset and changed on the instant into raw gold.

Maynard plucked a grass stem and chewed it reflectively, staring out across the purple moor and lazily watching the western sky turn from glory to glory. Over his head the smoke of the sacrifice still curled and eddied upwards. Then a sudden sound sent him on to one elbow—the thud of an approaching horse's hoofs.

"Moor ponies!" he muttered, and, rising, stood expectant beside his smoking altar.

Then he heard the sudden jingle of a bit, and presently a horse and rider climbed into view against the pure sky. A young girl, breeched, booted and spurred like a boy, drew rein, and sat looking down into the hollow.

For a moment neither spoke; then Maynard acknowledged her presence by raising his tweed hat. She gave a little nod.

"I thought it was somebody swaling—burning the heather." She considered the embers on the stone, and then her grey eyes travelled back to the spare, tweed-clad figure beside it.

He smiled in his slow way—a rather attractive smile.

"No. I've just concluded some pagan rites in connection with a small trout!" He nodded gravely at the stone. "That was a burnt sacrifice." With whimsical seriousness he told her of the trout's demise and high destiny.

For a moment she looked doubtful; but the inflection of breeding in his voice, the wholesome, lean face and humorous eyes, reassured her. A smile hovered about the corners of her mouth.

"Oh, is that it? I wondered . . ."

She gathered the reins and turned her horse's head.

"Forgive me if I dragged you out of your way," said Maynard, never swift to conventionality, but touched by the tired shadows in her eyes. The faint droop of her mouth, too, betrayed intense fatigue. "You look fagged. I don't want to be a nuisance or bore you, but I wish you'd let me offer you a sandwich. I've some milk here, too."

The girl looked round the ragged moor, brooding in the twilight, and half hesitated. Then she forced a wan little smile.

"I am tired, and hungry, too. Have you enough for us both?"

"Lots!" said Maynard. To himself he added: "And what's more, my child, you'll have a little fainting affair in a few minutes, if you don't have a feed."

74

"Come and rest for a minute," he continued aloud.

He spoke with pleasant, impersonal kindliness, and as he turned to his satchel she slipped out of the saddle and came towards him, leading her horse.

"Drink that," he said, holding out the cup of his flask. She drank with a wry little face, and coughed. "I put a little whisky in it," he explained. "You needed it."

She thanked him and sat down with the bridle linked over her arm. The colour crept back into her cheeks. Maynard produced a packet of sandwiches and a pasty.

"I've been mooning about the moor all the afternoon and lost myself twice," she explained between frank mouthfuls. "I'm hopelessly late for dinner, and I've still got miles to go."

"Do you know the way now?" he asked.

"Oh, yes! It won't take me long. My family are sensible, too, and don't fuss." She looked at him, her long-lashed eyes a little serious. "But you—how are you going to get home? It's getting late to be out on the moor afoot."

Maynard laughed.

"Oh, I'm all right, thanks!" He sniffed the warm September night. "I think I shall sleep here, as a matter of fact. I'm a gipsy by instinct—

> "'Give to me the life I love,
>   Let the lave go by me,
>   Give the jolly Heaven above—'"

He broke off, arrested by her unsmiling eyes. She was silent a moment.

"People don't as a rule sleep out—about here." The words came jerkily, as if she were forcing a natural tone into her voice.

"No?" He was accustomed to being questioned on his unconventional mode of life, and was prepared for the usual expostulations. She looked abruptly towards him.

"Are you superstitious?"

He laughed and shook his head.

"I don't think so. But what has that got to do with it?"

She hesitated, flushing a little.

"There is a legend—people about here say that the moor here is haunted. There is a Thing that hunts people to death!"

He laughed outright, wondering how old she was. Seventeen or eighteen, perhaps. She had said her people "didn't fuss." That meant she was left to herself to pick up all these old wives' tales.

"Really! Has anyone been caught?"

She nodded, unsmiling.

"Yes; old George Toms. He was one of Dad's tenants, a big purple-faced man, who drank a lot and never took much exercise. They found him in a ditch with his clothes all torn and covered with mud. He had been run to death; there was no wound on his body, but his heart was broken." Her thoughts recurred to the stone against which they leant, and his quaint conceit. "You were rather rash to go offering burnt sacrifices about here, don't you think? Dad says that stone is the remains of an old Phœnician altar, too."

She was smiling now, but the seriousness lingered in her eyes.

"And I have probably invoked some terrible heathen deity— Ashtoreth, or Pugm, or Baal! How awful!" he added, with mock gravity.

The girl rose to her feet.

"You are laughing at me. The people about here are superstitious, and I am a Celt, too. I belong here."

He jumped up with a quick protest.

"No, I'm not laughing at you. Please don't think that! But it's a little hard to believe in active evil when all around is so beautiful." He helped her to mount and walked to the top of the mound at her stirrup. "Tell me, is there any charm or incantation, in case—?" His eyes were twinkling, but she shook her fair head soberly.

"They say iron—cold iron—is the only thing it cannot cross. But I must go!" She held out her hand with half-shy friendliness. "Thank you for your niceness to me." Her eyes grew suddenly wistful. "Really, though, I don't think I should stay there if I were you. Please!"

He only laughed, however, and she moved off, shaking her impatient horse into a canter. Maynard stood looking after her till

76

she was swallowed by the dusk and surrounding moor. Then, thoughtfully, he retraced his steps to the hollow.

A CLOUD LAY ACROSS the face of the moon when Fear awoke Maynard. He rolled on to one elbow and stared round the hollow, filled with inexplicable dread. He was ordinarily a courageous man, and had no nerves to speak of; yet, as his eyes followed the line of the ridge against the sky, he experienced terror, the elementary, nauseating terror of childhood, when the skin tingles, and the heart beats at a suffocating gallop. It was very dark, but momentarily his eyes grew accustomed to it. He was conscious of a queer, pungent smell, horribly animal and corrupt.

Suddenly the utter silence broke. He heard a rattle of stones, the splash of water about him, realised that it was the brook beneath his feet, and that he, Maynard, was running for his life.

Neither then nor later did Reason assert herself. He ran without question or amazement. His brain—the part where human reasoning holds normal sway—was dominated by the purely primitive instinct of flight. And in that sudden rout of courage and self-respect one conscious thought alone remained. Whatever it was that was even then at his heels, he must not see it. At all costs it must be behind him, and, resisting the sudden terrified impulse to look over his shoulder, he unbuttoned his tweed jacket and disengaged himself from it as he ran. The faint haze that had gathered round the full moon dispersed, and he saw the moor stretching before him, grey and still, glistening with dew.

He was of frugal and temperate habits, a wiry man at the height of his physical powers, with lean flanks and a deep chest.

At Oxford they had said he was built to run for his life. He was running for it now, and he knew it.

The ground sloped upwards after a while, and he tore up the incline, breathing deep and hard; down into a shallow valley, leaping gorse bushes, crashing through whortle and meadowsweet, stumbling over peat-cuttings and the workings of forgotten tin-mines. An idiotic popular tune raced through his brain. He found himself trying to frame the words, but they broke into incoherent prayers, still to the same grotesque tune.

Then, as he breasted the flank of a boulder-strewn tor, he seemed to hear snuffling breathing behind him, and, redoubling his efforts, stepped into a rabbit hole. He was up and running again in the twinkling of an eye, limping from a twisted ankle as he ran.

He sprinted over the crest of the hill and thought he heard the sound almost abreast of him, away to the right. In the dry bed of a watercourse some stones were dislodged and fell with a rattle in the stillness of the night; he bore away to the left. A moment later there was Something nearly at his left elbow, and he smelt again the nameless, fœtid reek. He doubled, and the ghastly truth flashed upon him. The Thing was playing with him! He was being hunted for sport—the sport of a horror unthinkable. The sweat ran down into his eyes.

He lost all count of time; his wrist watch was smashed on his wrist. He ran through a reeling eternity, sobbing for breath, stumbling, tripping, fighting a leaden weariness; and ever the same unreasoning terror urged him on. The moon and ragged skyline swam about him; the blood drummed deafeningly in his ears, and his eyeballs felt as if they would burst from their sockets. He had nearly bitten his swollen tongue in two falling over an unseen peat-cutting, and blood-flecked foam gathered on his lips.

God, how he ran! But he was no longer among bog and heather. He was running—shambling now—along a road. The loping pursuit of that nameless, shapeless Something sounded like an echo in his head.

He was nearing a village, but saw nothing save a red mist that swam before him like a fog. The road underfoot seemed to rise and fall in wavelike undulations. Still he ran, with sobbing gasps and limbs that swerved under his weight; at his elbow hung death unnamable, and the fear of it urged him on while every instinct of his exhausted body called out to him to fling up his hands and end it.

Out of the mist ahead rose the rough outline of a building by the roadside; it was the village smithy, half workshop, half dwelling. The road here skirted a patch of grass, and the moonlight, glistening on the dew, showed the dark circular scars of the turf where, for a generation, the smith's peat fires had heated the great iron hoops that tyred the wheels of the wains. One of these was even then lying on the ground with the turves placed in readiness for firing in the morning, and in the throbbing darkness of Maynard's consciousness a voice seemed to speak faintly—the voice of a girl:

"There's a Thing that hunts people to death. But iron—cold iron—it cannot cross."

The sweat of death was already on his brow as he reeled sideways, plunging blindly across the uneven tufts of grass. His feet caught in some obstruction and he pitched forward into the sanctuary of the huge iron tyre—a spasm of cramp twisting his limbs up under him.

As he fell a great blackness rose around him, and with it the bewildered clamour of awakened dogs.

DR. STANMORE CAME DOWN the flagged path from the smith's cottage, pulling on his gloves. A big car was passing slowly up the village street, and as it came abreast the smithy the doctor raised his hat.

The car stopped, and the driver, a fair-haired girl, leant sideways from her seat.

"Good-morning, Dr. Stanmore! What's the matter here? Nothing wrong with any of Matthew's children, is there?"

The Doctor shook his head gravely.

"No, Lady Dorothy; they're all at school. This is no one belonging to the family—a stranger who was taken mysteriously ill last night just outside the forge, and they brought him in. It's a most queer case, and very difficult to diagnose—that is to say, to give a diagnosis in keeping with one's professional—er—conscience."

The girl switched off the engine, and took her hand from the brake-lever. Something in the doctor's manner arrested her interest.

"What is the matter with him?" she queried. "What diagnosis have you made, professional or otherwise?"

"Shock, Lady Dorothy; severe exhaustion and shock, heart strained, superficial lesions, bruises, scratches, and so forth. Mentally he is in a great state of excitement and terror, lapsing into delirium at times—that is really the most serious feature. In fact, unless I can calm him I am afraid we may have some brain trouble on top of the other thing. It's most mysterious!"

The girl nodded gravely, holding her underlip between her white teeth.

"What does he look like—in appearance, I mean? Is he young?"

The shadow of a smile crossed the doctor's eyes.

"Yes, Lady Dorothy—quite young, and very good-looking. He is a man of remarkable athletic build. He is calmer now, and I have left Matthew's wife with him while I slip out to see a couple of other patients."

Lady Dorothy rose from her seat and stepped down out of the car.

"I think I know your patient," she said. "In fact, I had taken the car to look for him, to ask him to lunch with us. Do you think I might see him for a minute? If it is the person I think it is I may be able to help you diagnose his illness."

Together they walked up the path and entered the cottage. The doctor led the way upstairs and opened a door. A woman sitting by the bed rose and dropped a curtsey.

Lady Dorothy smiled a greeting to her and crossed over to the bed. There, his face grey and drawn with exhaustion, with shadows round his closed eyes, lay Maynard; one hand lying on the counterpane opened and closed convulsively, his lips moved. The physician eyed the girl interrogatively.

"Do you know him?" he asked.

She nodded, and put her firm, cool hand over the twitching fingers.

"Yes," she said. "And I warned him. Tell me, is he very ill?"

"He requires rest, careful nursing, absolute quiet—"

"All that he can have at the Manor," said the girl softly. She met the doctor's eyes and looked away, a faint colour tingeing her cheeks. "Will you go and telephone to father? I will take him back in the car now if he is well enough to be moved."

"Yes, he is well enough to be moved," said the doctor. "It is very kind of you, Lady Dorothy, and I will go and telephone at once. Will you stay with him for a little while?"

He left the room, and they heard his feet go down the narrow stairs. The cottage door opened and closed.

The two women, the old and the young, peasant and peer's daughter, looked at each other, and there was in their glance that complete understanding which can only exist between women.

"Do 'ee mind old Jarge Toms, my lady?"

Lady Dorothy nodded.

"I know, I know! And I warned him! They won't believe, these men! They think because they are so big and strong that there is nothing that can hurt them."

"'Twas th' iron that saved un, my lady. 'Twas inside one of John's new tyres as was lyin' on the ground that us found un. Dogs barkin' wakened us up. But it'd ha' had un, else—" A sound downstairs sent her flying to the door. "'Tis the kettle, my lady. John's dinner spilin', an' I forgettin'."

She hurried out of the room and closed the door.

The sound of their voices seemed to have roused the occupant of the bed. His eyelids fluttered and opened; his eyes rested full on the girl's face. For a moment there was no consciousness in their gaze; then a whimsical ghost of a smile crept about his mouth.

"Go on," he said in a weak voice. "Say it!"

"Say what?" asked Lady Dorothy. She was suddenly aware that her hand was still on his, but the twitching fingers had closed about hers in a calm, firm grasp.

"Say 'I told you so'!"

She shook her head with a little smile.

"I told you that cold iron—"

"Cold iron saved me." He told her of the iron hoop on the ground outside the forge. "You saved me last night."

She disengaged her hand gently.

"I saved you last night—since you say so. But in future—"

Someone was coming up the stairs. Maynard met her eyes with a long look.

"I have no fear," he said. "I have found something better than cold iron."

The door opened and the doctor came in. He glanced at Maynard's face and touched his pulse.

"The case is yours, Lady Dorothy!" he said with a little bow.

THE TRAGEDY AT THE *LOUP NOIR*
GLADYS STERN

THE BOY AT THE CORNER of the table flicked the ash of his cigar into the fire.

"Spiritualism is all rot!" he declared.

"I don't know," the Host reflected thoughtfully. "One hears queer stories sometimes."

"Which reminds me—" started the Bore.

But before he could proceed any further the little French Judge ruthlessly cut him short.

"Bah!" Contempt and geniality were mingled in his tone. "Who are we, poor ignorant worms, that we should dare to say 'is' or 'is not'? Your Shakespeare, he was right! 'There are more things in heaven and earth, Horatio, than are dreamt of in your philosophy!'"

The faces of the four Englishmen instantly assumed that peculiarly stolid expression always called forth by the mention of Shakespeare.

"But Spiritualism—" started the Host.

Again the little French Judge broke in:

"I who you speak, I myself know of an experience, of the most remarkable, to this day unexplained save by Spiritualism, Occultism, what you will! You shall hear! The case is one I conducted professionally some two years ago, though, of course, the events which I now tell in their proper sequence, came out only in the trial. I string them together for you, yes?"

The Bore, who fiercely resented any stories except his own, gave vent to a discontented grunt; the other three prepared to listen carefully. From the drawing-room, whither the ladies had retired after dinner, sounded the far-away strains of a piano. The little French Judge held out his glass for a crème de menthe; his eyes were sparkling with suppressed excitement; he gazed deep into the shining green liquid as if seeing therein a moving panorama of pictures, then he began:

On a dusky autumn evening, a young man, tall, olive-skinned, tramps along the road leading from Paris to Longchamps. He is walking with a quick, even swing. Now and again a hidden anxiety darkens his face.

Suddenly he branches off to the left; the path here is steep and muddy. He stops in front of a blurred circle of yellow light; by this can one faintly perceive the outlines of a building. Above the narrow doorway hangs a creaking sign which announces to all it may concern that this is the "Loup Noir," much sought after for its nearness to the racecourse and for its excellent *ménage*.

"*Voilà!*" mutters our friend.

On entering, he is met by the burly innkeeper, a shrewd enough fellow, who has seen something of life before settling down in Longchamps. The young man glances past him as if seeking some other face, then recollecting himself demands shelter for the night.

"I greatly fear—" began the innkeeper, then pauses, struck by an idea. "Holà, Gaston! Have monsieur and madame from number fourteen yet departed?"

"Yes, monsieur; already early this morning; you were at the market, so Mademoiselle settled the bill."

"Mademoiselle Jehane?" the stranger looks up sharply.

"My niece, monsieur; you have perhaps heard of her, for I see by your easel you are an artist. She is supposed to be of a rare beauty; I think it myself." Jean Potin keeps up a running flow of talk as he conducts his visitor down the long bare passages, past blistered yellow doors.

"It is a double room I must give you, vacated, as you heard, but this very morning. They were going to stay longer, Monsieur and Madame Guillaumet, but of a sudden she changed her mind. Oh, she was of a temper!" Potin raises expressive eyes heavenwards. "It is ever so when May weds with December."

"He was much older than his wife, then?" queries the artist, politely feigning an interest he is far from feeling.

"*Mais non, parbleu!* It was she who was the older—by some fifteen years; and not a beauty. But rich—he knew what he was about, giving his smooth cheek for her smooth louis!"

Left alone, Lou Arnaud proceeds to unpack his knapsack; he lingers over it as long as possible; the task awaiting him below is no pleasant one. Finally he descends. The small smoky *salle à manger* is full of people. There is much talk and laughter going on; the clatter of knives and forks. At the desk near the door, a young girl is busy with the accounts. Her very pale gold hair, parted and drawn loosely back over the ears, casts a faint shadow on her pure, white skin. Arnaud, as he chooses a seat, looks at her critically.

"Bah, she is insignificant!" he thinks. "What can have possessed Claude?"

Suddenly she raises her eyes. They meet his in a long, steady gaze. Then once again the lids are lowered.

The artist sets down his glass with a hand that shakes. He is not imaginative, as a rule, but when one sees the soul of a mocking devil look out, dark and compelling, from the face of a Madonna, one is disconcerted.

He wonders no more what had possessed Claude. On his way to the door a few moments later, he pauses at her desk.

"Monsieur wishes to order breakfast for to-morrow morning?"

"Monsieur wishes to speak with you."

She smiles demurely. Many have wished to speak with her. Arnaud divines her thoughts.

"My name is Lou Arnaud!" he adds meaningly.

"Ah!" she ponders on this for an instant; then: "It is a warm night; if you will seat yourself at one of the little tables in the court-yard at the back of the house, I will try to join you, when these pigs have finished feeding." She indicates with contempt the noisily eating crowd.

They sit long at that table, for the man has much to tell of his young brother Claude; of the ruin she has made of his life; of the little green devils that lurk in a glass of absinthe, and clutch their victim, and drag him down deeper, ever deeper, into the great, green abyss.

But she only laughs, this Jehane of the wanton eyes.

"But what do you want from me? I have no need of this Claude. He wearies me—now!"

Arnaud springs to his feet, catching her roughly by the wrist. He loves his young brother much. His voice is raised, attracting the notice of two or three groups who take coffee at the iron tables.

"You had need of him once. You never left him in peace till you had sucked him of all that makes life good. If I could—"

Jean Potin appears in the doorway.

"Jehane, what are you doing out here? You know I do not permit it that you speak with the visitors. Pardon her, monsieur, she is but a child."

"A child?" The artist's brow is black as thunder. "She has wrecked a life, this child you speak of!"

He strides past the amazed innkeeper, up the narrow flight of stairs, and down the passage to his room.

Sitting on the edge of the huge curtained four-poster bed, he ponders on the events of the evening.

But his thoughts are not all of Claude. That girl—that girl with her pale face and her pale hair, and eyes the grey of a storm cloud before it breaks, she haunts him! Her soft murmuring voice has stolen into his brain; he hears it in the drip, drip of the rain on the sill outside.

Soon heavy feet are heard trooping up the stairs; doors are heard to bang; cheery voices wish each other good-night. Then gradually the sounds die away. They keep early hours at the "Loup Noir"; it is not yet ten o'clock.

Still Arnaud remains sitting on the edge of the bed; the dark plush canopy overhead repels him, he does not feel inclined for sleep. Jehane! what a picture she would make! He *must* paint her!

Obsessed by this idea, he unpacks a roll of canvas, spreads it on the tripod easel, and prepares crayons and charcoal; he will start the picture as soon as it is day. He will paint her as Circe, mocking at her grovelling herd of swine!

He creeps into bed and falls asleep.

85

SOFTLY THE RAIN PATTERS against the window-pane.

A distant clock booms out eleven strokes.

Lou Arnaud raises his head. Then noiselessly he slides out of bed on the chill wooden boarding. As in a trance he crosses the room, seizes charcoal, and feverishly works at the blank canvas on the easel.

For twenty minutes his hand never falters, then the charcoal drops from his nerveless fingers! Groping his way with half-closed eyes back to the bed, he falls again into a heavy, dreamless slumber.

THE EARLY MORNING SUN chases away the raindrops of the night before. Signs of activity are abroad in the inn; the swish of brooms; the noisy clatter of pails. A warm aroma of coffee floats up the stairs and under the door of number fourteen, awaking Arnaud to pleasant thoughts of breakfast. He is partly dressed before his eye lights on the canvas he had prepared.

"Nom de Dieu!"

He falls back against the wall, staring stupefied at the picture before him. It is the picture of a girl, crouching in a kneeling position, all the agony of death showing clearly in her upturned eyes. At her throat, cruelly, relentlessly doing their murderous work, are a pair of hands—ugly, podgy hands, but with what power behind them!

The face is the face of Jehane—a distorted, terrified Jehane! Arnaud recoils, covering his eyes with his hands. Who could have drawn this unspeakable thing? He looks again closely; the style is his own! There is no mistaking those bold, black lines, that peculiar way of indicating muscle beneath the tightly stretched skin—it *is* his own work! Anywhere would he have known it!

A knock at the door! Jean Potin enters, radiating cheerfulness.

"Breakfast in your room, monsieur? We are busy this morning; I share in the work. Permit me to move the table and the easel—*Sacré-bleu!*"

Suddenly his rosy lips grow stern. "This is Jehane. Did she sit for you—and when? You only came last night. What devil's work is this?"

"That is what I would like to find out; I know no more about it than you yourself. When I awoke this morning the picture was there!"

"Did you draw it?" suspiciously.

"Yes. At least, no! Yes, I suppose I did. But I—"

Potin clenches his fist: "I will have the truth from the girl herself! There is something here I do not like!" Roughly he pushes past the artist and mounts to Jehane's room.

She is not there, neither is she at her desk. Nor yet down in the village. They search everywhere; there is a hue and cry; people rush to and fro.

Then suddenly a shout; and a silence, a dreadful silence.

Something is carried slowly into the "Loup Noir." Something that was found huddled up in the shadow of the wall that borders the courtyard. Something with ugly purple patches on the white throat.

It is Jehane, and she is dead; strangled by a pair of hands that came from behind.

The story of the picture is rapidly passed from mouth to mouth. People look strangely at Lou Arnaud; they remember his loud, strained voice and threatening gestures on the preceding night.

Finally he is arrested on the charge of murder.

I WAS THE JUDGE, gentlemen, on the occasion of the Arnaud trial.

The prisoner is questioned about the picture. He knows nothing; can tell nothing of how it came there. His fellow-artists testify to its being his work. From them also leaks out the tale of his brother Claude, of the latter's infatuation and ruin. No need now to explain the quarrel in the courtyard. The accused has good reason to hate the dead girl.

The Avocat for the defence does his best. The picture is produced in court; it creates a sensation.

If only Lou Arnaud could complete it—could sketch in the owner of those merciless hands. He is handed the charcoal; again and again he tries—in vain.

The hands are not his own; but that is a small point in his favour. Why should he have incriminated himself by drawing his own hands? But again, why should he have drawn the picture at all?

87

There is nobody else on whom falls a shadow of suspicion. I sum up impartially. The jury convict on circumstantial evidence, and I sentence the prisoner to death.

A short time must elapse between the sentence and carrying it into force. The Avocat for the defence obtains for the prisoner a slight concession; he may have picture and charcoal in his cell. Perhaps he can yet free himself from the web which has inmeshed him!

Arnaud tries to blot out thought by sketching in and erasing again fanciful figures twisted into a peculiar position; he cannot adjust the pose of the unknown murderer. So in despair he gives it up.

One morning, three days before the execution, the innkeeper comes to visit him and finds him lying face downwards on the narrow pallet. Despite his own grief, he is sorry for the young man; nor is he convinced in his shrewd bourgeois mind of the latter's guilt.

"You *must* draw in the second figure," he repeats again and again. "It is your last, your only chance! Think of the faces you saw at the 'Loup Noir.' Do none of them recall anything to you? You quarrelled with Jehane in the garden about your brother. Then you went to your room. Oh, what did you think in your room?"

"I thought of your niece," responds Arnaud wildly. "How very beautiful she was, and what a model she would make. Then I prepared a blank canvas for the morning, and went to bed. When I woke up the picture was there."

"And you remember nothing more—nothing at all?" insists Jean Potin. "You fell asleep at once? You heard no sound?"

Against the barred window of the cell the rain patters softly. A distant clock booms out eleven strokes.

Something in the artist's brain seems to snap. He raises his head. He slides from the bed. As in a trance he crosses the cell, seizes a piece of charcoal, and feverishly works at the picture on the easel!

Not daring to speak, Jean Potin watches him. The figure behind the hands grows and grows beneath Arnaud's fingers.

A woman's figure!

Then the face: a coarse, malignant face, distorted by evil passions.

"Ah!"

It is a cry of recognition from the breathless innkeeper. It breaks the spell. The charcoal drops, and the prisoner, passing his hand across his eyes, gazes bewildered at his own work.

"Who? What?"

"But I know her! It is the woman in whose room you slept! She was staying at the 'Loup Noir' the very night before you arrived, and she left that morning. She and her husband, Monsieur Guillaumet. But it is incredible if *she* should have—"

I will be short with you, gentlemen. Madame Guillaumet was traced to her flat in Paris. Arnaud's Avocat confronted her with the now completed picture. She was confounded—babbled like a mad woman—confessed!

A reprieve for further inquiry was granted by the State. Finally Arnaud was cleared, and allowed to go free.

The motive for the murder? A woman's jealousy. Monsieur and Madame Guillaumet had been married only ten months. Her age was forty-nine; his twenty-seven. Every second of their married life was to her weighted with intolerable suspicions; how soon would this young husband, so dear to her, forsake her for another, now that his debts were paid? It preyed upon her mind, distorting it, unbalancing it; each glance, each movement of his she exaggerated into an intrigue.

On their way to Paris they stayed a few days at the "Loup Noir"; Charles Guillaumet was interested in racing. Also, he became interested in a certain Mdlle. Jehane. Madame, quick to see, insisted on an instant departure.

The evening of the day of their departure she missed her husband, and found he had taken the car. Where should he have gone? Back to the inn, of course, only half-an-hour's run from Paris. She hired another car and followed him, driving it herself. It was not a pleasant journey. The first car she discovered forsaken, about half-a-mile distant from the inn. Her own car she left beside it, and trudged the remaining distance on foot.

The rest was easy.

Finding no sign of Guillaumet in front of the house, she stole round to the back. There she found a door in the wall of the courtyard—a door that led into the lane. That door was slightly ajar. She slipped in and crouched down in the shadow.

Yes, there they were, her husband and Jehane; the latter was laughing, luring him on—and she was young; oh, so young!

The woman watched, fascinated.

Charles bade Jehane good-bye, promising to come again. He kissed her tenderly, passed through the gate; his steps were heard muffled along the lane.

Jehane blew him a kiss, and then fastened the little door.

A distant clock boomed out eleven strokes, and a pair of hands stole round the girl's throat, burying themselves deep, deep in the white flesh.

"AND THE HUSBAND, was he an accessory after the fact?" inquired the Boy.

"Possibly he guessed at the deed, yes; but, being a weakling, said nothing for fear of implicating himself. It wasn't proved."

The Host moved uneasily in his chair.

"Do you mean to tell me that the mystery of the picture has never been cleared up?" he asked. "Could Arnaud have actually seen the murder from his window, and fixed it on the canvas?"

The little French Judge shook his head.

"Did I not tell you that his window faced front?" he replied. "No, that point has not yet been explained. It is beyond us!"

He made a sweeping gesture, knocking over his liqueur glass; it fell with a crash on the parquet floor.

The Bore woke with a start.

"And did they marry?" he queried.

"Who should marry?"

"That artist-chap and the girl—what was her name?—Jehane."

"Monsieur," quoth the little French Judge very gently and ironically, "I grieve to state that was impossible, Jehane being dead."

The Boy at the corner of the table stood up and threw the stump of his cigar into the fire.

"I think Spiritualism is all rot!" he declared.

THE MAILED FOOT
HERMINA BLACK AND EDITH BLAIR-STAPLES

I

THE ROOM IN THE EAST WING

IN SPITE OF MY MODEST SUCCESS in journalism I am not an imaginative person. I can only manage to tell this story because the events are too vividly impressed upon my mind for me ever to forget them.

In December of ninety-eight I was on my own in London, rather depressed and run down and looking forward to a lonely Christmas, when I unexpectedly ran across Owen Flaxham. We were at Magdalen together, where he was my special pal, but somehow when I came to town and took up scribbling and he came in for the baronetcy, we lost sight of each other—which was more the fault of circumstances than of either of us.

Anyway, he was delighted to meet me again, and, on hearing that I was spending my Christmas alone, insisted that I should accompany him home the following day. I couldn't do that, but I promised to follow him during the week. Accordingly I left Euston on Friday, arriving at Monorsfield in Cheshire some time after dark.

Owen met me with a dog-cart, and we had a drive of six miles before we reached the house. On the way up I gathered, rather to my discomfort, that the place was packed; my host apologetically asked me if I would mind turning in with him for that night as the man who had my room was leaving in the morning. Of course I had no objection, and told him so.

Flaxham Hall was a big, rambling sort of place, Elizabethan with the exception of the east wing, which was all that remained of what the building had originally been, and dated back to the tenth century. The house possessed some of the finest oak panelling it has been my lot to see, and was the ideal setting for a hundred ghost stories—the idea flashed into my head as I unpacked my bag, while Owen sat on one of the beds in his big, cheerful bedroom, and I turned to him laughingly, inquiring if they possessed a family spook.

He nodded.

"Yes—only for heaven's sake don't refer to it before the women! The Mater's rather nervy just now. I'll tell you about it later if you'll remind me."

And, changing the subject, he proceeded to explain the difficulty they had had in installing electric light throughout the huge place.

"There is only one part of the house without it now," he finished. "But as there is only a single bedroom in the east wing, which is very seldom used, it really doesn't matter. As a matter of fact, that room happens to be the one which, after to-night, you are going to occupy—a bit rough on you, old man!"

"I don't mind," I retorted cheerfully. "I've never cultivated the vice of reading in bed, and when I'm once asleep I doubt if an earthquake would wake me."

I found Owen's mother a delightful *grande dame* of the old school. His sister, Mrs. Dawson, was a member of the party, and I thought at once what an awfully pretty woman she was. But even on that first evening I noticed she seemed unhappy and ill at ease whenever her husband—who was a rich and delightful American— came near her. There was one other person who seemed uncomfortable—a lanky youth boasting the name of Mundy, who I afterwards found had occupied the room I was to have. But I never got a chance of speaking to him before he left—later I thought he might have had something illuminating to say.

II

PERIL INVISIBLE

NEXT DAY WE WERE OUT shooting from early morning. Owen's man moved my things from his master's room to my new quarters, and when I got in I found him waiting to escort me thither. One needed

92

a guide, too! The room was quite apart from the rest of the sleeping accommodation. One had to traverse the whole length of the picture gallery before one reached it, and after dark the gallery was a weird enough place, lit as it was, at intervals, by dimly burning oil lamps, with portraits of dead and gone Flaxhams gazing solemnly down on one, and huge suits of armour looming out of the gloom. At the very end a short flight of stone steps led downwards to a small, square passage, and directly opposite an oak door studded thickly with nails gave access to my sleeping apartment. Seeing it, I ceased to wonder at the timid Mundy's discomfort—for it was horribly isolated.

The room itself was comfortable enough, with a blazing fire in the grate and plenty of big, wax candles in huge silver sticks burning on the mantel-piece and the big, old-fashioned dressing-table. Warm, red curtains were drawn over the high windows, and these, combined with a crimson carpet and a couple of comfortable armchairs, helped to dispel the gloom of the heavy oak furniture, and the great four-poster which stood against the wall in one corner with three steps leading up to it.

I dismissed the man, and he seemed extraordinarily pleased at the idea of getting away. At the door he paused.

"'Ope you'll be comfortable, sir—you'll find plenty more candles there if you want them"—pointing to a box on a side-table.

I thanked him and he took himself off—I heard him hurrying through the gallery, and couldn't help laughing at the rate at which he seemed to be going.

Left alone, I remember glancing at the bed and thinking I should probably prefer to sleep on one of the chairs, but I had not much time for thought as the first gong had sounded some time back, and I had to rush into my clothes.

When, after another jolly evening, I at length sought my lonely quarters it was past midnight. The fire was still burning cheerily, all the candles were lit, and I found Davis busy putting my things ready for the night. To my intense amusement, placed on a table near the fire was a tray containing whisky and soda, three or four magazines and an evening paper.

93

"Looks as though you thought I was going to make a night of it, Davis," I remarked.

He explained with an air of absolute guilt:

"Well, it's a very cold night, sir—and Mr. Mundy, sir, 'e complained of the chilliness of the room—said 'e found it difficult to sleep—so I thought maybe you'd like a drink and a book or two. Anything else you want, sir?"

There was nothing, so Davis went off with the same alacrity I had observed earlier. He turned back once at the door, opened his mouth as though to speak, appeared to think better of it, and bidding me a respectful "good-night," vanished.

As I undressed slowly I couldn't help wondering what lay at the back of the man's rather strange behaviour, but as yet I cannot say I was in the least uneasy. Having got into my pyjamas, I mixed myself a drink, swallowed half of it, and putting down my glass, picked up a candle and went over to examine the bed. It seemed all right—high, but comfortable, and I decided to patronise it after all. Then, as I descended from beside it, my eyes happened to fall on my watch, which I had placed on the dressing-table, and I saw that the hands pointed to one. At the same moment one boomed from the stable clock.

Now, it's a very funny thing, for I hadn't read "Hamlet" for years, but as the clock struck there suddenly flashed into my mind those very unpleasant words of the old bard's:

> "'Tis now the witching hour of night,
>   when churchyards yawn—"

I found myself repeating it, when suddenly I heard someone coming along the gallery.

My first thought was that either Davis was returning or Owen was coming to have a final chat, but I quickly grasped that the footfall was too heavy for either of them. I put down the candle I held and stood listening. The steps came on—measured, heavy; and as they drew nearer there was a distinct clang, just as though one of the old suits of armour that decorated the gallery was taking a

94

midnight ramble. Still not nervous, and by this time sure that some mad fool downstairs had donned one of the suits of mail and contemplated playing a practical joke on me, I crossed to the door, softly locked and bolted it, and waited.

The footfall approached steadily; then, as it reached the steps and came down them with a clang of metal, I was aware that I had somehow got into the middle of the room. To this day I have no recollection of moving.

It was as if a mailed fist struck the door; without any warning the candles on the mantel-piece went out, and I found myself flat upon the floor, face upwards and unable to move hand or foot. At the same moment I knew that I was no longer alone.

Though I knew I had locked the door, making it impossible for anyone to come in, there It was—and there was I, unable to move, not in the least alarmed, but devilishly annoyed! I could not turn my head, but I knew that whatever had entered was standing near the door, and that It was looking at me intently. Then It began to move—deliberately—round the room.

I realised vaguely that, whatever its purpose, It was at present keeping almost against the wall, and not in the least impeded by the furniture. I lay and wondered, but strain my eyes as I would, I could see nothing. Then I understood what my visitor was doing. He—or It—whichever you like—was walking round and round the room slowly and in ever-smaller circles, for each time It reached the door I felt the presence nearer to me. Though by this time I felt distinctly uneasy, I had no feeling that my visitor was in the least antagonistic to me.

Then, as It drew nearer and nearer, the sweat began to ooze from my pores, for I had a sudden horrible idea that It was standing beside me and contemplating stamping on my face. I held my breath, expecting every moment that a mail-encased foot would descend and crush me. There was a movement almost as though it were lifted for that purpose. Then to my amazement It turned and walked towards the door.

It went the way It had come, echoing and dying away along the gallery. After it came a silence—intense, deadly; then to my relief I found that I could move. Springing to my feet I rushed to the door—it was still locked and bolted. For the first time my nerves got the better of me—I dared not look out to pursue that unknown horror.

I dared not even put out the remaining candles, so I got hastily into bed and lay for some time listening for the return of my ghostly visitant. Then I dropped asleep and was awakened by Davis' voice announcing my shaving water.

III

AN UNWELCOME GUEST

GETTING UP, I unlocked the door. The man came in, drew back the curtains, and with a deprecating glance at me inquired:

"Sleep well, sir?"

In the cold light of the December morning my experience of last night seemed absurd and impossible. I felt that to speak of it would be to have my sanity questioned so I replied cheerfully that I *had* slept very well, which seemed to relieve him. Having by this time placed everything to his satisfaction, he left me to my dressing.

Bathed, shaved, and dressed, the events of last night receded more than ever. The experience I had undergone seemed such an absolute impossibility that I grew more and more certain I had eaten something which had caused a bad attack of indigestion, and so brought about the nightmare through which I had passed. In fact, it seemed so silly that I decided not to speak of it to a soul. I must have looked pretty bad though, for my hostess—herself pale and apparently not in the easiest frame of mind—remarked on my appearance with solicitude, inquiring if I had slept badly, and if I were sure that I found the room comfortable. Somehow it suddenly flashed across me that she had a very shrewd idea of what actually was the matter, and it was on the tip of my tongue to ask her when I remembered Owen's request and held my tongue. I told her I had slept fairly well, and, with the same relief I had noted in Davis, she turned to the perusal of her morning's mail. She and Owen and I were the only people at the breakfast-table—the others having gone off skating.

Presently my hostess handed a letter across to her son with a rather worried glance.

"From Godfrey, dear—he is coming down to-day!"

Owen frowned.

"The deuce he is! Where are you going to put him?"

She hesitated.

"There is not a room vacant—I am afraid he will have to go in with you."

Owen's frown deepened.

"I call it pretty cool of him to turn up like this! He might guess we'd be full up—I've half a mind to wire and put him off!"

"I don't quite see how we could do that," his mother replied gently, though she seemed no more pleased than he at the advent of this unexpected guest.

Flaxham glanced at the letter he held with a vexed laugh.

"No more do I—the blighter hasn't even given us an address!"

She rose, gathering together her letters.

"That settles it, then. He will have to come, and he must make the best of our lack of accommodation." And with that she left the room.

Flaxham remained, moodily knocking his spoon against his empty coffee-cup. After a moment's hesitation I said:

"You don't seem overpleased at the prospect of this uninvited guest, old man."

"I'm not," he retorted frankly. "To tell you the truth, George, he's a sort of cousin of ours—a man I can't stick at any price. He'll turn up with his man and a pile of luggage, and treat the place as though it belonged to him."

It was then that an overwhelming impulse prompted me to say:

"Why not let him have my room? I don't mind where you put me."

The words were out almost before I knew it, but Owen looked at me with relief in his eyes.

"That's awfully good of you, George, but it seems a shame to turn you out again. Of course, you'd come back to me—I'd miles rather have you share my room than Godfrey, if you really don't mind?"

"Not a bit," I cut in. "Only too delighted—I'll go and get my things together now." But he assured me Davis would see to all that and went away to tell his mother what we had arranged, leaving me delighted at the chance of clearing out of that uncanny room. I tried to soothe my conscience by the fact that even had my nocturnal visitor been an actuality he was quite harmless—with the exception of jarring one's nerves rather. Besides, there was almost the chance that it had been nothing but a dream, though somehow this theory didn't seem to wear very well. For a moment I did think of telling Owen, but I decided I should only be laughed at for my pains. Afterwards I could not help feeling that a mightier power than mere fear of ridicule sealed my lips.

IV

UNDERCURRENTS

ABOUT TEA-TIME Mr. Godfrey Leyton arrived. He was one of the best-looking fellows I've ever set eyes on—big and broad-shouldered, with dark, curling hair—but he'd a beastly cruel mouth. Almost as soon as he arrived he went over and seated himself beside Mrs. Dawson—we were all gathered in the great, oak-panelled hall, Lady Flaxham dispensing tea—and kept her in more or less intimate conversation for some time. I thought she seemed ill at ease with him, though once or twice I caught them exchanging glances that, if I'd been Dawson, I should have taken decided objection to. I couldn't help wondering if the estrangement between husband and wife had anything to do with this very prepossessing cousin.

After dinner that evening I left the others to their bridge and their games and retired to the study—a small room at the back of the library to write a letter which I particularly wished to catch the morning's post. I was feeling jumpy and off colour and had a beastly headache, no doubt the result of my disturbed night. Anyway, I didn't feel much like returning to the crowd in the hall; so, having finished my letter, I switched off the light and, selecting a comfortable arm-chair, prepared for a quiet smoke.

I must have dozed off, for when I woke, though the room was still in darkness, I was aware of two other occupants besides

98

myself. I was just about to call out to know who was there when a woman's voice exclaimed:

"What do you want, Godfrey? You're making me most unhappy! Suppose my husband should come?"

"No fear of anyone coming in here if we don't put on the light," replied her companion—and I realised that it was Mrs. Dawson and young Leyton.

Here was a nice situation! Whatever they had to say to each other had no interest for me, but I had paused long enough to make them imagine I was deliberately eavesdropping. I decided to remain where I was, sticking my fingers in my ears, until they chose to go on their way, but before I had time to do this Leyton spoke again, and his tone made me decide to listen. I always have had a soft spot for a damsel in distress.

"As for unhappiness, Cecily, you have caused me enough. I came down here especially to have a talk with you."

"It was most unkind of you" she interrupted. "You know that ever since Jack found that letter of yours he has suspected me. Please, Godfrey, go away to-morrow! You are only making things worse."

"It was about your letters that I wanted to see you, Cecily. You wrote asking me—"

"Yes, yes!" she exclaimed eagerly. "You did as I asked? You destroyed them?"

He answered at once: "No," and at that she gave a frightened little cry. He seemed to take her hands and try to comfort her—the cad! I could willingly have kicked him! After a moment he resumed:

"You can't expect me to part easily with all that I have left of you—but see here, dear, I promise faithfully to give every one back to you if you will come for them yourself."

"But how can I?" she asked breathlessly.

"Meet me in the picture gallery to-night, an hour after they've all gone to bed," he replied. "I'll give them to you then and you can destroy them. After that—well, I swear that I will go away to-morrow—if you still wish it."

At first she refused outright. But I could hear from her tone how anxious she was to regain those confounded letters, and after

99

a time she promised to do as he asked. They were just leaving the room when Mrs. Dawson paused, adding something that really caused me to prick up my ears. There was terror in her voice.

"But I simply dare not come into the picture gallery at that hour. Oh, Godfrey, be careful! Do you know you have the end room?" And, as he laughed outright: "Wait—the Mailed Foot is walking! My mother has heard it, and last night I heard it, too. Even the servants have complained of strange noises from the east wing. You may laugh, but I am afraid."

"Nonsense!" he exclaimed. "Who believes those old wives' tales? If you want your letters you must come for them."

She renewed her promise, though in a very subdued manner, and to my intense relief they went away, leaving me feeling like a criminal.

For the rest of the evening the recollection of what I had over-heard worried me considerably. Somehow I felt that I ought to warn Flaxham, for I knew that I. could do no good by talking to Mrs. Dawson herself. What I couldn't make out was whether she was really keen on Leyton or just frightened of him, but I was certain that up to the present things had gone no further than a rather desperate flirtation. I knew the type of man Leyton was, though, and I did not like that appointment. Anyway, the poor little fool would compromise herself hopelessly by keeping it—and yet what right had I to interfere?

V

THE LEGEND

IT WAS JUST ON TWELVE when we all retired for the night and, remembering that Mrs. Dawson was not due in the picture gallery until an hour after the house had betaken itself to rest, I decided with some satisfaction that Leyton would probably have been visited by my unknown friend in armour before that. If my summary of his character were in any way correct he would not venture out of his room before daylight to keep any sort of tryst. To tell the truth, I thought a good, wholesome fright would do him no harm.

Neither Flaxham nor I was very sleepy. Having got into our dressing-gowns we established ourselves in the comfortable arm-chairs on either side of the fireplace, and, lighting our pipes, settled down for a pow-wow. We chattered about old times for a while, and had lapsed into silence, smoking contentedly, when I suddenly made up my mind to ask him to tell me the legend which he had hinted at on the evening of my arrival. He didn't speak for a time; then removing his pipe he knocked out the ashes and proceeded to refill it, saying slowly:

"No reason why I shouldn't tell you. You know most old families are supposed to have their spooks, George, and we Flaxhams are not a fortunate exception. Only we don't talk about ours, because it rakes up stories that the family would rather forget. Outside the family there are very few people who have heard of the Mailed Foot."

This brought me straight up in my chair.

"Go on!" I urged eagerly.

Flaxham smiled.

"I can't say that I personally pay much heed to these things. I have to see a thing or at least have some tangible proof of it before I believe in its existence, and I can't say that I have ever seen this particular apparition, though even now there are those in the house who swear to having heard it, at least. The legend goes back as far as the days of Richard the First when the Hall was a Norman keep, and the second holder of the title—Sir Edward Flaxham—reigned here. All that remains of that building now is the east wing—where you slept last night.

"Well, Sir Edward, so the story runs, had 'one fair daughter whom he loved passing well'—in other words, she was a deucedly pretty girl and the apple of his eye. But two things came before her—his King and his honour. He was a perfect stickler for honour.

"After a time the old fellow got the crusading craze, and off he went to ye holie war, leaving his lovely daughter to the care of her ladies and the trusty retainers—for her mother was dead. He was away in the Holy Land for a dickens of a time, and you can imagine what he felt like when, on his return, he found that his daughter Edith had died by her own hand rather than face the disgrace brought upon her by a certain knight.

101

"Sir Edward swore to find the man and be revenged—firstly because he loved his daughter, and secondly because the honour of the family demanded it, for the Flaxham women were renowned for their virtue. After a time he discovered his enemy. He had the young man seized and brought to the Hall, where he imprisoned him in that room at the end of the picture gallery. It has a stone floor—I hope you didn't find it cold, old man!—and to that the prisoner was fastened by heavy chains.

"Now the story has it that, when the lover of Edith was at last brought to the keep, Sir Edward was just off to the crusades again. Late that night he visited his prisoner, attired in a full suit of mail, and walking round the room informed him quietly that when he reached him he was simply going to crush the life out of him. I can't remember what his exact words are supposed to have been, but they ran to the effect that his handsome face had done enough damage, and that he—Sir Edward—was now going to spoil it. So he walked round and round that big, almost empty room, while the other unfortunate devil was fastened to the floor, face upwards, and unable to move hand or foot. My noble ancestor walked on, always in narrowing circles, until, coming up to his victim, he very deliberately raised one of his mailed feet and just stamped the life out of him."

"Good God!" was all I could get out just then.

"Quaint idea, wasn't it?" inquired Flaxham. "Now the superstition runs that whenever the honour of one of the Flaxham women is in jeopardy, Sir Edward is heard to walk. And if he can get at the right man he will do to him just what he did to his daughter's betrayer."

"But," I cried breathlessly, "has that ever been known to happen? I mean—"

"Well," said Owen, with a sudden access of seriousness, "the funny part of the business is that three or four times men are supposed to have been found in that room dead by some unknown agency, and with their faces crushed out of all recognition—as though they had been stamped on by a steel-clad foot. The last case was in the eighteenth century, when handsome Denis Hallam was found there. It afterwards came out that on the very night of his death he was to have eloped with Lady Betty Flaxham, wife of the then reigning baronet. They said that for nights before he slept in that room the footsteps had been heard. The idea is that the ghost will only harm the betrayer or would-be betrayer of a woman of the family."

I don't know why in heaven's name it had not struck me earlier, but at his words my mind suddenly swung back to the conversation I had overheard in the study, and my experience in the room at the end of the picture gallery took new and sinister form. It was born upon me that at any cost I must get to Godfrey Leyton and warn him before one o'clock struck, for he was in deadly danger.

Then, while I remained in momentary doubt as to how it would be best to move, the big grandfather clock outside the door struck one. In a second I was on my feet.

"Owen!" I cried, clutching him by the arm. "For God's sake come with me to the picture gallery—quickly, man!"

I darted towards the door and wrenched it open, but before I could get out Flaxham had seized hold of me. He told me afterwards he had serious doubts as to my sanity.

"Hold hard, old man!" he reasoned, keeping a tight grip of me. "What on earth's wrong?"

"I haven't time to go into explanations now. I am quite sane. For the love of heaven, ask no questions but come with me at once!" I urged. "Leyton is in that end room, and he is in danger—I know it!"

The gravity of my tone convinced him I was in earnest, and as he let me go I caught up a candlestick, and hurried into the passage, putting a match to the wick as I walked. Flaxham followed close upon my heels urging me to explain more fully.

Heedless of his importunities I hurried on in silence until we had turned from the more modern wing of the house and reached the staircase which led upwards to the picture gallery. The lights had long since been extinguished, and as I passed between the rows of armoured figures lining the stairs my excitement began to cool and uneasiness to take its place. I waited at the stair-head—ostensibly to regain my breath, and Owen caught up with me. Then, as we paused, the long, dark gallery stretching before us, I distinctly heard the clang of armour.

VI

THE MARK OF THE AVENGER

FOR THE FIRST TIME, the sound of the Mailed Foot filled me with real fear. I had had it in the same room with me, close enough to do me bodily harm but never once had it raised in me the dread which it raised as I heard it echoing along the deserted picture gallery before me. Mastering my horror with a mighty effort I caught hold of my companion and dragged him along.

"Do you not hear it?" I demanded. But there was no need for an answer, for I caught a glimpse of his face in the flickering light of the candle I bore. He had caught my mood and was as eager as I to gain the room where Leyton slept, and into which, but a moment since, we had heard the footsteps pass.

Then an unlooked for thing happened. As we reached the short flight of steps which led downstairs to the nail-studded door, we both found we were incapable of further movement. There we stood, regarding each other helplessly, I holding the guttering candle in one hand, while all the time we could hear the movement in the room not half-a-dozen yards away. I knew that at any moment a terrible and appalling tragedy would be enacted behind that closed door, and I was powerless to utter a cry or stretch forth a finger to prevent it. The pacing footsteps went on, heavily insistent.

It had never struck me that the ghost might have identically the same effect on anyone outside the room as within. We stood there, our brains the only portion of us fully alive, for, I should think, five minutes. Then suddenly a woman's scream pierced the silence and flying footsteps rushed along the gallery.

In my eagerness I had forgotten Cecily Dawson, but I realised at once it was she. As she caught sight of us standing there motionless she called to her brother desperately:

"Owen, Owen, for God's sake, go on—go in! Don't you hear? Godfrey is in there! Go in to him one of you—oh, for the love of Heaven!"

She reached us, came between us, a desperate, slight figure in a soft dressing-wrap. As she caught her brother's arm silence fell within the room.

Almost immediately the steps came towards the door. I had barely time to catch the fainting girl in my arms, and draw back close against the wall, when something brushed past me—and I swear I felt the hardness and coldness of steel against my hands!

When that brief silence fell it had released us from the spell of immovability, but the rest had happened so swiftly that we had no time to realise our regained freedom of action. As I caught Mrs. Dawson I had dropped my candle, which had gone out.

We two men stood there in the darkness, I holding my unconscious burden. We could hear the throbbing echo of the footsteps as they died away. The room was away from all the other rooms. Then I felt Flaxham's shaking hand upon my arm.

"I must go in," he said. "Leave her here and come with me."

Laying my unconscious burden gently down I followed him. He found the latch of the door and, opening it, passed in before me. One candle was burning on the mantel-shelf. He walked towards it, stumbled over something on his way and, stooping, called to me to bring more light.

Enough to say that I obeyed him. The thing he had tripped over was the body of Godfrey Leyton, and as I stooped to put the candle near we saw that he was lying on his back.

His face was crushed out of all recognition. Horrible! Horrible!

No one except Flaxham, myself, and the family doctor saw Leyton after. It was given out that he had died of heart failure.

THE PIPERS OF MALLORY
HENRIETTA D. EVERETT (AS THEO. DOUGLAS)

I

WHILE MY LAST LETTER was flying out to you in India, dear Margaret, and your reply flying back to me, a great deal has been happening.

My last letter was all about Jack, wasn't it?—how we met and fell in love and how he was under orders for the war, and so we had to be married in a desperate hurry—such a hurry that it shocked Aunt Winifred, glad as she was to get rid of me.

I told you what I was going to wear, and Jack says I made rather a nice-looking bride (he put it more strongly than that). He was, of course, in khaki, and looked dearer than ever, and half an hour or less turned me into Mrs. Frazer. We had only nine days for our honeymoon instead of the three weeks we hoped for, but they were nine lovely days. Then there was the dreadful going away; but, before that came about, the question had to be settled—the question you ask, my dear cousin—what was to become of me while Jack was away in France fighting those horrible Huns?

It was over this Jack and I had our first difference—not a serious difference, for we kissed and made it up at once—when I found out what he wanted me to do. He actually wished me to make my home with his mother in Scotland—fancy that—to bury myself for months and months in the wilds with a woman I did not know, who would be worse than Aunt Winifred twice over. I had never been free in my life, but always in leading-strings, and I made up my mind I would be free now, quite on my own, to make up for what I should suffer through Jack being away.

I didn't tell Jack that—about wanting to be emancipated, he would not have understood. I told him what was quite true—that I wanted to make my V.A.D. training of use, and do war work of sorts in a London hospital, like Violet Power. And my plan was that Violet and I should take a flat together, a tiny flat, which would cost next to nothing (I thought), near enough to her hospital to be convenient, a hospital which needed helpers, and would find work for me, too.

Jack did not like it. Dear fellow! He is one of the old-fashioned sort who thinks women should be hedged about and protected, and give themselves up to looking after their household concerns; but he gave in when he saw I was determined.

That was nearly at the end of our time together—our lovely time. He had planned to take me up to Mallory, to say good-bye at the end of his leave, but having to go off suddenly altered that. However, he made me promise I would go there alone as soon as he left, to pay my mother-in-law a long visit before I settled down with Violet in the flat. Over that I was obliged to yield (with some private reservation about the long), for, as you will understand, I could not say "No" to him just then.

Well, we parted, and it was a hard parting. He put me in the night train for the North, before he left to cross over to France. Peters, his mother's servant, was to meet me in Edinburgh and take care of me from there; you see, I could not get away from the "take care."

Now you will know from my letter, the "Jack" letter, that I had never seen Lady Heron. She is always more or less of an invalid, and bronchitis, or something like that, prevented her taking the long journey to be present at our wedding. Fancy having attacks of bronchitis, and yet living up there in the North! She has been a widow for many years, and Jack is her only son; there is a son by a former marriage, Jack's half-brother, who is now Lord Heron. The Frazers are poor in these days, but Jack's mother has an income of her own, though I do not think it is a large one. Mallory is the old family place—mind you pronounce it right—*Mal*-lory, and not the other way. I suppose Lady Heron would not live there if Heron married, but he is still a bachelor, and with the regiment somewhere in France.

Jack does not say much about his half-brother. I fancy the two are not very good friends.

Peters was waiting for me on the Edinburgh station, and by that time I was feeling rather better, and able to take an interest in what was new. Breakfast was ready for me at an hotel, with no bill for it, as Peters paid everything. I was "her leddyship's guest," he said, and it was by Lady Heron's orders; he seemed quite hurt when I offered. A very good breakfast it was, and I was hungry, for I had been far too wretched to eat any dinner the night before. Then, after rest and refreshment, I had to sally forth again to a different station, Peters carrying my hand-luggage. And when we gained the street—that wonderful street with the Castle opposite, standing up grey against the morning sky—there was a skirl of wild music coming towards us, with the tramp of marching feet.

A skirl. That is the right word for bagpipes, as perhaps you know. I daresay you have heard them in India, as there are Scottish regiments there, but I had never heard them before. Their music may be barbaric—people say so; but there is something about it that fires the blood—that fired my blood, though I am only a Scotswoman married and not born. I could understand how it put spirit into the tired feet which were following, muddy from a long route march, as they kept time to the swing and beat of the brave tune. Jack belongs to a Highland regiment, of course, the same that Heron is in. And at the moment I felt prouder than ever to be Jack's wife.

"I suppose Lady Heron has a piper at Mallory, has she not?"

It was the first question I had put to Peters. I had the notion that a piper must be a necessary appendage to every Highland family of importance; Lady Heron would not of course detain a young man, but she might so employ some old retainer, past the age to be of service in the war. But the servant shook his head. He, too, is quite elderly—did I say?—and speaks broad Scotch, though his name might as well be English.

"No, mom," he answered, "we hef no piper at Mallory. Her leddyship does not like the pipes."

Not like the pipes! How odd of her, I thought. And upon this scrap of information the latent opposition which I had felt towards Jack's mother from the beginning swelled and took shape. How strange of a woman who had soldier sons—a son and a step-son—and who wrote as if she were proud of them and their calling; and of one who I knew from Jack was Highland bred to the backbone!

Throughout the journey north-west, now with great hills looming up through mist, now by the side of rushing streams, I was thinking of my mother-in-law, and how much easier it would have been to meet her for the first time if Jack had gone with me to Mallory. I was afraid of her, to tell the truth, and that made me brace myself beforehand to be defiant, picturing a great lady who would stand on her dignity, and think Jack might have done better for himself than in marrying me, an Englishwoman of no particular family and small fortune. She would condemn, she would dictate, she would want to interfere.

The day wore on; the train was not a fast one, and there were frequent stoppages, and every hour Peters would come to the window to know whether I wanted anything. But at last there came the station where we alighted for Mallory.

There was a car to meet us, and in less than half an hour Mallory came into view. Not the fine place I had been picturing to myself, only a moderate-sized country house, but possessing a tower with corner-turrets in the Scottish fashion, which gives it some distinction. The rest of the house is low, with thick walls of undoubted antiquity. The windows are small, but beyond them there are lovely views.

It was only a confused impression I derived from that first entrance—of a hall warm with firelight, decorated with heads of beasts, and skins and weapons, of a room beyond, also warm, and of a frail little lady rising from her chair at the window, and coming lamely across to greet me with an embrace and a kiss.

Such a frail little lady to be the mother of a great, strong man like Jack She, like the house, was not what I expected, but I was right in two particulars. She is *grande dame* to the finger-tips, and I am certain she views me critically.

ON FURTHER ACQUAINTANCE I like Lady Heron better than I expected, and I have been able to express myself somewhat enthusiastically in writing to Jack; this will please him. I would give a good deal to know what her letter—the long letter I saw her writing—said to him about me. She is kind to me, painstakingly kind, but still we are strangers to each other, and I think it likely we shall be strangers to the end. That she is fond of Jack ought to knit a bond between us, but somehow I strongly suspect it is the very thing which holds us apart.

She is always testing and appraising me, though not in the way I expected; she tells me little anecdotes of Jack's youth, and watches to see if I receive them with the enthusiasm I ought; she shows me some cherished pictures—stupid, old-fashioned photographs—of Jack as a baby, Jack as a toddler learning to walk, and upwards at various stages of his boyhood. It is plainly my duty to care about these, but I don't particularly; they seem too far removed from the Jack I know. The pictures bore me, and I shudder inwardly when a new anecdote is presented. And, sitting here in the chair of truth, I must confess it—I find Mallory dull.

My chief amusement is going out for rambles by myself, rambles Lady Heron is too lame to share; she can only walk up and down the terrace with her stick by way of exercise, and that at the sunniest time of the day. The surroundings here are certainly beautiful, and the Highland people interest me. I talk to them when I have a chance, and try to get accustomed to their way of speech. It was from one of these Highlanders I found out the reason why Lady Heron does not like the pipes.

I never put the question to her. I do not know why not, as it would have been a simple thing to ask, but whenever it came into my head, something happened to divert the thought and keep the words unspoken. But that thrilling pibroch heard in Edinburgh seemed to haunt me here at Mallory, though not always the same tune. I dreamt of it the first night I was here; it waked me from sleep, as a real thing might have done but when I listened in the deep, country stillness and the darkness of the unfamiliar room, there was not a sound. And each time I walked in the direction of Glen Fruin I heard it with my waking ears, very faint and far in the distance, but I could be certain it was there.

I went some way up the Glen on the third occasion, hoping to get nearer to the sound, but it seemed to recede as I approached; the preliminary skirl, and two or three bars of a tune, as if the musician were practising, and then a fault and silence. Presently my watch warned me I should return, for Mallory is a punctual household, and Lady Heron would be waiting tea. I was well on my way home when I met an old shepherd I had spoken to before, and, as I still heard the music at intervals, I bethought myself to ask him:

"Who is it about here who plays the pipes? Somebody is practising away there in the Glen."

Highland fashion, he met my question by another, and his shaggy brows drew together.

"You be the leddy Frazer, be you not?"

I was Mrs. Frazer, I told him.

"Eh, weel, ye are Frazer married, and so have a right to hear. 'Tisn't lucky for the Frazers when the pipes are sounding in Glen Fruin, but the Lord be thankit that they don't come lower down! I do not look to hear them mysel', being nobbut Steenson that was once Macgregor."

This was pretty well Greek to me.

"Why isn't it good for the Frazers?" I demanded.

"Ye've never heard the legend? Mebbe 'tis not for the likes of me to tell ye, but seeing as ye ask— Time gone by the chief of the Frazers had his pipers equal with the best, always seven of them in his tail, and callants growing up to take the place—and a proud place it was—of them as were short-winded or old. Glen Fruin was full of folk in those days, where there's nought now but a wheen ruins, or a square in the green to mark where walls have been. And custom was that Frazer's pipers should be chosen from the Glen Fruin folk.

"That was a time of battles, same as now, and the Frazers were up in arms. I don't mind the name of the battle, no, nor how long

111

ago, but there was a great slaughter, and the Frazers fell to a man, and the pipers with their chief. It is said there was none to fill their places, for the callants had not been instructed, and the head of the clan was nobbut a wailing Cairn. And since that day the Frazers have had no pipers—the Frazers of Mallory. Mebbe that is why the dead men are not content, and when a Frazer is about to die they are heard piping in Glen Fruin."

I am putting down the old man's words as nearly as I remember them, but I daresay I spell them wrong. As I listened a cold shiver went down my spine and crept among the roots of my hair; if my hair had been undone I think it would have stood up with fright.

"Why, you don't mean to say," I stammered—"you don't mean to tell me that what I have been hearing is a ghost? A ghost in broad daylight and in the open air! And who is it who is going to die?"

"You needn't be afeared, my leddy, for him as is your own. There's a many Frazers at the war besides, and the pipers pipe the same for a death in bed. There's John Frazer near his end at the Mill, and mebbe 'tis for him. He has a son fighting, and Donald Frazer, farmer, has two more. Ye need na fear for the heads of the clan, or for their womenfolk, unless the pipers come right down to Mallory, and go round the house."

"Do they come as close as that?" I asked, shuddering.

"Ay, my leddy, that they do. And they are heard by all of the Frazer name, and sometimes by them as are not so called, but I never heard tell of their being seen. It is just a sound and no more, sometimes a lament on the pipes, sometimes a fine march for them as fall. And they go once round for a woman, and twice for the heir, and three times for the head of the clan. They went three times round the house when the late lord died, and there was many who heard them, together with my Leddy Heron hersel'. And ever since then she hasna been able to bear the pipes, the real pipes, and they are warned not to come nigh."

After that I wondered no more at what Peters had told me in Edinburgh. The faint, far-off skirling, which had sounded even while old Steenson was speaking, ceased as I hurried back, but Mallory looked a dark blot in the prospect, dismal as it had never seemed before. Was it because of this superstition that Lady Heron had grown old and grey before her time? It would be awful, I thought, to live here year in and year out, eternally listening for those notes of doom. What should I do, I, a married Frazer, if I heard them circling round the house, and if it meant that Jack—

I tell you frankly what was my first impression afterwards; some healthy scepticism came to my relief. An old man's story of impossible ghosts—where was the need to credit it?

Through that day and the next everything moved on velvet—the quiet, regular hours, the careful service, the slightly formal ways with an old-world atmosphere about them, which I found piquant and attractive when not in one of my impatient moods. And I was perhaps more patient, more inclined to be appreciative, because the weeks of my visit had nearly run out; very soon now I should be setting out to establish myself with Violet at the flat, in the midst of London and life.

I was softened, too, because Lady Heron appeared to recognise my right of choice as to what I would do in Jack's absence. All she said was:

"Your home is here, my dear, when you care to have it so. When you wish to come back to Mallory you have only to let me know."

Then I heard her sigh softly to herself, perhaps because she recognised that I did not care. I thanked her and said I would write, and she replied:

"I think I shall know without telling." An odd thing to say.

On the next evening, which was the last but one, we were sitting together in the half-light with the windows open, for although it was late October the weather was still warm. I was holding wool for Lady Heron to wind, and was so close in front of her and could clearly see her face, when, in the distance, and a mere thread of sound, but perfectly distinct, I heard the skirl of the pipes.

I do not think my hands trembled, held out stiffly with the skein, but hers did in the effort to wind. The thin, faint music came near, nearer, and then seemed to turn away. Not to the house; for all my cherished unbelief, I was thankful that it was not coming to the house.

Lady Heron had dropped her ball of wool, and now stooped to regain it.

"We will not wind any more now, my dear," she said. "I am obliged to you, but I shall have enough." And then she crossed the room and rang the bell, a hanging bell-pull, old-fashioned like all else at Mallory. Peters came quickly; was it only my fancy that he looked disturbed

"We will have the windows closed now and the lamp lit." Such was her commonplace order. I heard no more of the pipes that night, but next morning came the news that John Frazer, the tenant of the Mill, had passed away.

It was no doubt a coincidence, nothing more, but we may put it down as an odd one. That was the day before yesterday. I left early yesterday morning, Peters going with me as far as Edinburgh, and I have been busy writing, writing, all these hours in the train. What a packet you will have to wade through!

III

YOU HAVE BEEN GOOD, dear Margaret, in liking my letters about the hospital work, although while I was so busy they could only be scraps. (And, what was worse, I am afraid my letters to poor old Jack in the trenches were scrappy too. Ungrateful, perhaps, for I have lived all this while on his scraps to me.)

But to go back to the hospital. You will be surprised to hear that I have had to give up my work there, which is a great disappointment. But everything has been horrid of late. I am alone in the flat. The beginning of the upset was that Violet turned horrid; wasn't it nasty of her, when we had been such chums? I told you about Captain Bridgwater, who used to come to see us after he left the hospital; he was cousin to some of Violet's people, and an old schoolfellow of Jack's. It seemed right and natural to be friends, as that was so I liked him in the beginning—really I liked him very much, and was pleased when he showed that he liked me. But Violet liked him in a different way, and expected a flirtation they had begun years before to have a serious meaning; she declares it would have meant something serious if it had not been for me. So we had a quarrel, and she said dreadful things, and I was indignant, as I had a right to be, and was not sorry when she packed her boxes and gave up her share of the flat, leaving me alone.

. I was not sorry, but I was shaken by it, and it so happened that when Captain Bridgwater came in he found me crying. Then he was horrid, too, and said things—things that at first I did not understand, and that he had no business to say to Jack's wife, he who had been Jack's friend. I shall never speak to him again, you may be sure.

After this I went to the hospital, to my work as usual, but I did not feel a bit like myself. I had a fainting fit for the first time in my life, and they were a long while in bringing me to. Afterwards the doctor told me I should have to give up V.A.D.-ing. I am not strong enough.

I am wondering what I ought to do. Jack would not like me being here by myself. He only consented to the plan because Violet was joining me, and I do not know of anybody else. But nothing on earth will induce me to go back to Aunt Winifred.

I WAS INTERRUPTED THERE, and now where do you think I am continuing my letter? I am writing in the train, the Scotch express, and I am on my way to Mallory. There is a surprise for you, and a surprise for me, but I begin to think it is the best solution of the difficulty that could have been found. Lady Heron sent for me, and the queer thing is how she could have known or guessed. I begin to think my mother-in-law must be a bit of a witch.

Where I broke off above was when the servant came in to say a man named Peters had called and had brought a letter. It was a kind letter, so kind a letter that it made me cry, though that is saying little, as tears have been close to my eyes of late. The rigours of winter were past, Lady Heron wrote; the days were already lengthening into spring; a visit would give her the utmost pleasure, and she fancied it might now suit me to come to her again. Peters was her messenger instead of the post, and if I were willing Peters would arrange my journey, and spare me all trouble about it, as indeed he has done. And it was not necessary for me to write. Peters would send her a wire, and a warm welcome would await me.

So here I am travelling North. And I think you will agree it has been a wise decision, and one that will please Jack as things are. I shall post this to you in Edinburgh, my dear, and write again from Mallory.

IV

REALLY, MARGARET, I am happy to be here, much happier than I was before. Lady Heron is so kind, and I think we understand each other better than we did. I have a lovely room on the south side of the house, and the air is far milder than you would suppose. We never say anything about the pipes, but I fancy they must have been heard twice at least while I was in London, because two more of the Frazers have fallen; sons of the people at the farm; and another of the clan name died in hospital the week before my return.

ALAS! WE HAVE HEARD the pipes again, and I will tell you how. They came at the edge of dusk, not what they call here the murk of the night, but while there was still light enough to see, had there been bodily presence to be seen.

Lady Heron likes me to play to her, and I was sitting at the piano, recollecting old airs, and sometimes crooning a bit of song half to myself, when it seemed as if my music had an echo outside the house. My fingers fell from the keys, and in another moment I was sure what it was, and where.

It came with a sweep, swiftly, devouring space, heard afar, and then immediately close, passing our window, which looked out upon nothing—nothing, not a shadow even, nor the print of a foot. The wild pibroch passed by, but it went circling round the house, and, oh, it was coming back? We both sprang up and met in a close clasp together, each of us calling the other by name. "Mother!" I cried to her—the first time I have called her so, but it seemed rent from me without thought. It passed the second time, and now there was a cry with it, like a human voice in pain, and again it went circling through the air which had been still, but was rising with a gust of storm.

116

Twice for the heir! That was what the old man Steenson said, and, oh, me! Jack was the heir. There was a pause of seconds, and then it passed for the third time, the pibroch and the shriek. Afterwards there was a great silence. The wind which had swept with it fell also—if it were wind indeed; and we two women drew apart and looked at each other. Her face was ghastly, and I expect mine was no better.

"Cecily," she said, "you know!" And then, "Who told you?"

Soon afterwards Peters came in to light the lamps, and the old servant's hands so trembled as he performed his task that the glasses clashed and clattered—he who was usually noiseless. He, too, had heard; of that I made no doubt; he had heard even as we.

It was the sign for the head of the house. Lady Heron heard it just so before her husband died. There was some small comfort to us both in the belief that it came for Heron and not Jack. But that comfort did not last. The telegram from the War Office came two days after—"*Wounded and missing, believed killed*"—the intimation to Lady Heron about both her sons, Lieut.-Colonel Lord Heron, and Captain the Hon. John Frazer; not one alone, but both.

I cannot write about that time. A chink was left to us through which hope came, but one could hardly look at it in face of the awful doubt. And the sign for the head of the house would stand also for Jack, provided Heron had been the first to fall.

V

LOOKING BACK I cannot think how we endured the suspense. Counted by days the measure of it was not long, but it seemed as if ages went by. We tried to comfort each other; Lady Heron was an angel to me through all her own pain; but for her I would have died.

I cannot write about it; you must take it for granted, and I hurry on to the end. We were sitting together, we two alone, as we were when the sign came. Lady Heron was knitting, feverishly knitting at those socks for Jack which she would not lay aside, little as either of us believed they would be worn. We were together, as I said, when Peters rushed into the room with another telegram on his silver tray. (I wonder he remembered the tray.) Lady Heron tore it open; it was addressed to her. *"Home slightly wounded. With you and Cecily to-morrow.—Jack."*

My mind takes a leap from that moment to another when he stood at the door. Lady Heron would not let me go to the station because I had fainted again, and as I might not, she would not either; she said it would be unfair to take the advantage. Jack at the door, a figure in soiled khaki, very pale, with his head bandaged and his arm in a sling; Jack himself, alive and still to live. My Jack; and I do not mind now, as once I did, that he is his mother's Jack as well.

He has been through dreadful things. Heron fell—poor Heron— and was left in No Man's Land, and Jack went after him. At the utmost risk to himself he dragged out his brother from under a pile of dead, and into the shelter of a shell-crater. There they existed for three days under incessant fire, all hope of them being abandoned; existed by a miracle, for it was death to move. Heron was fearfully wounded, but Jack, wounded himself, managed so to bandage him that the bleeding stopped; and then he found some emergency rations on which they sustained life. If there ever were a coldness between the brothers, as I thought, it must have melted away in those dreadful hours.

On the fourth day our troops attacked again on the farther side of the wood, which diverted attention, and then Jack began the task—the difficult and painful task—of half-carrying, half-dragging Heron to where he could be helped, as his only chance of life. All this time Jack was wounded himself, in the head and on the shoulder and side, but the burst of shrapnel which shattered his arm did not happen till they were close to our own lines. By this Heron was wounded again, but in any case Jack thinks he could not have survived; the doctor at the dressing-station said so. Heron died there, but not till some hours later, and Jack was with him to the last.

So the pipers were right and not wrong when they bewailed the head of the house who had fallen. What it meant to Jack I did not consider then, and it came on me with a shock of surprise when Peters, some time later, addressed him as "my lord."

But I think more—much more—of the fact that he has been recommended for the Cross.

VISITING ROUNDS
MICHAEL KENT

BEFORE HE JOINED UP Raymond Holt had been the bright star of the Modern Theatre. He did not join up very quickly, however, for the value of his productions, which included Cubist scenery, neurotic plot, and a certain morbidity of tone seemed to him of greater national importance than the gift of his nerve and sinew in the services of his country. Moreover, the amount of nerve and sinew which he had to offer was not considerable.

Eventually, however, he went to the Crystal Palace and embraced a life of action. The change, mainly a consequence of the vulgar preference for *revue* over modern art, stirred Raymond to the depths of his soul. He got his hair cut—a bitter sacrifice. He learnt much about the position of his hands and feet which was totally at variance with stage tradition, and he earned a valuation of his general intelligence and real worth as painful to himself as it would have been to the patrons of the Modern Theatre. On the other hand, his arms, legs, and chest increased in a manner that was neither morbid nor neurotic, and, in spite of a certain dismay at this, he felt a real satisfaction at the first small expressions of approval from his C.P.O. The Chief Petty Officer drew his notions of art from the Mile End Borough Theatre, and had an idea that Futurism was some sort of religion.

Yet Raymond, for all these signs of grace, was not happy. He did not love his heritage of heavy boots and scratchy underclothing. He hated his hard, dirt-stippled palms. So when, after many tribulations, an avenue of escape opened, he promptly took it and became a lieutenant. This would not have been possible in the ordinary course, but many things happened out of the ordinary course in those days.

Raymond's new life was certainly easier. He was second in command of His Majesty's Ship *Recorder*, the same being a half-acre of cinder-heaps enclosed within a quarter of a mile of corrugated-iron fencing, some impressive barbed-wire entanglements, one searchlight, one gasolene engine for same, and a high-angle gun. The good ship *Recorder* rode securely at anchor between a glue factory and a dump for old iron in a dingy suburb of London, whose name must never be revealed.

Raymond had studied many strange things to attain this desired haven—angles and arcs, and fields of fire, and Morse signalling. As may be supposed, he had a good memory, and that gave him a start over the untrained. Yet even here there was a thorn in the flesh—his commander, a heavy-jowled, blue-nosed old sea-dog who had spent the best years of his active career in pushing an iron-skinned auxiliary gunboat round the Northern Pacific. The fact that Commander Ballantyne had only one eye, had led the Lords of the Admiralty to deny him a place on blue water despite historical precedent, and he had to be content with the cinder-heap. He was not. Add to this the fact that he was a martinet, suffering landsmen grimly and despising every form of art, and it may be imagined that Raymond's thorn was poignant enough in all conscience.

The Commander quickly decided that for Raymond the only hope of salvation lay in ragging. He ragged him accordingly with an elephantine irony.

"What a jolly, hail-fellow-well-met young dog you are, to be sure," he said to him coming off parade one morning.

"Why?" asked Raymond cautiously.

"Well," returned Ballantyne, "didn't I hear you address the port watch on parade as 'dear laddies'? You'll be darning their socks for 'em next."

Of course the "Second" was not entirely expert in his work. One night in spring as Ballantyne was going off, he heard him, as officer of the watch, speak to the look-out.

"What's the light, Simmons, bearing right over the church tower?"

Ballantyne took out his watch. It was a quarter to eight. He put his head in at the office door. "Take down, logsman," he said, "15.45 O.C." (so runs the time in the service) "*Officer of the watch reports strange light bearing W.S.W.*"

The report was duly logged, and the Commander lingered on the station another five minutes filling his pipe.

"What's come to your light, Holt?" he asked anxiously, as he prepared to go.

"Still there, sir," replied Raymond, "southing a little."

"Keep an eye on it," said Ballantyne drily, and went. On his return to quarters he went straight to the log and read:

"*16.12 O.C. Light reported at 15.45 O.C. by Lieut. Holt and confirmed by Cr. Ballantyne proves to be the Dog Star.*"

"'*Confirmed by Commander Ballantyne,*'" quoted the Skipper wrathfully. "As if I don't know Sirius when I see it! The young cub must know that I only had it logged to teach him a lesson."

Later on the papers started a "slackers" campaign, and the Commander conceived it his duty to point out to Holt that an anti-aircraft station in the R.N.A.S. involved little physical strain and no risk to a man well under forty.

"There's many a slacker in khaki and Navy blue," he remarked once sententiously.

"You're right there, sir," returned Holt with hearty innocence.

In a moment the Commander tried again.

"I say, Holt," he said, "I've often wondered you don't transfer into something a bit more active."

"I've thought about it myself," said Holt lazily.

"How about the M.P.?" asked the Senior. "I could get you a job on the Motor Patrol any day you like."

Ballantyne, as a fact, would have gone on his knees to anyone who would have taken Holt off the ship's books of the *Recorder*.

"Oh, I could never stand the M.P.," drawled Holt. "If I changed into anything at all it would be the Flying Corps."

Ballantyne laughed short and sharp.

"Want to see your picture in the *Daily Snapshot* bringing down a Zepp?" he asked sardonically.

"You've hit it, sir," said Holt. "This craze for notoriety which bites the great lights of the drama! Gets into the blood, what?" He knew that would rile his senior; any reference to the stage always did.

"Huh!" said Ballantyne. "It's a different sort of limelight you have to perform under up yonder." He jerked his thumb skywards. "You haven't the nerve for it, my lad."

"Perhaps I haven't," returned Holt, with irritating philosophy.

"You bet you haven't," said the Commander, and Raymond Holt's lazy eyes opened wide.

"Oh," he said rather sharply. "If it's betting, what do you put on it, sir?"

"Put on what?" asked Ballantyne,

"On my nerve. What d'you bet I don't take a star part? What d'you bet I don't bring down a Zepp from the sky before you touch one from the ground?" Raymond Holt seemed awake at last.

The Commander looked at him but made no reply.

"Any odds you like," went on Holt. "Here you are; my motorcycle to your fountain-pen. How's that, sir?"

Ballantyne wrinkled his brows a moment, then: "That's a cheap cycle," he said. "I'll take you on—always provided you get into the Service."

And so it was.

Lieutenant Holt passed from the view of H.M.S. *Recorder*, and his old life saw him no more. Instead he donned khaki, went to Salisbury Plain, and was rushed through a course of training which left him at the end with two silvery-looking wings outspread upon the left breast of his plastron tunic.

As a matter of fact Holt made rather a good airman. There was something about that high nerve tension—the swift swoops through space, the sense of holding one wide, empty stage seen and wondered at by all—that reminded him of his old life and his former triumphs. It rejoiced him to hold his life cheap; as, in the old days, it shocked the conventions. The delicate, nervous sympathy which had made him famous in his art gave him an uncanny understanding of all those high-strung, trembling, indicator fingers which now ministered to him. With just that same skill which before he had used to play on human hearts, he played on his fierce, fragile cylinders and the wild winds of the sky. Men whose business it was to watch the brood of fledglings marked him as a likely bird, and he found himself, at the end of four months, back in London with a different *rôle* to play.

Now the *Recorder* had followed its daily routine through spring to summer. As the days began to shorten they found headquarters starting to call them up at unearthly hours and bid them stand by till dawn.

So the Zepp season came in with long periods of waiting for all hands braced and steady in the blind night, while the engine buzzed and the engineer conned his clocks, and the men stood ready on the light to fling their ten thousand candle-power into the menacing dark.

One night a little before twelve (23.52 O.C. it appears on the log) they were called up from headquarters. They had waited thus a bare half-hour when they caught the buzz of aircraft engines high above. The Admiralty rang through again, passing on the news gleaned by the little dot-lights busy in the sky.

"Zepp in Q.14 making W.N.W."

"Ready to cut in," signalled the man on the light, a full circle with his flash lamp.

"Elevation 46," the man on the range-finder spoke through to the gun.

"All lights on," called mother in Whitehall to her children in every suburb.

"All on," sang the Commander joyously to the light.

"One, two, three," whispered the man on the switch to himself, counting the seconds, and threw the arm over.

On a sudden, as the *Recorder's* beam shot up, the heavens split in jets and arms of light ready centred upon Q.14, and there, blinded in the apex of bright, crisscrossing rays, lay the foe, a small, ribbed opal in the vivid night. A moment more there was silence, while every range-finder swung his sighting wires on to the object; then for three minutes every gun roared into the air its stream of shells as quick as hand could swing the breech-block home, as swift as No. 1 could correct his errant fire. Up above the Zepp seemed dizzy, swaying, in the tempest she evoked, then up she went into the higher air; yet still the *Recorder's* light hung on to her. Others would have lost her, but Ballantyne himself had taken the two great handles and, while the sweat poured from his face, and grim, unheard curses from his lips, he held his light upon the fleeing foe.

Suddenly a red flare glowed above the great balloon, and every gun was still.

The old known drama was being played again. David had gone forth, his sling was swinging in his hand, and Goliath knew not where to hold his shield. Followed the glow, the blaze of white-hot metal shreds, the great radiance over earth while men shouted, and the night closed in upon the raider's last grim voyage to land.

Not all men shouted, however, for there were some who watched to see within that ruby glow the emerald flares that told of David's safety.

They did not find them.

On board the *Recorder* the hands still stood by, for they had not yet had the call from the Admiralty to make all fast. The whole company then was at stations, and the sentry on the outer gate was Seaman Lovyer.

About ten minutes after the fall of the Zepp, a shadow came silently up the path towards the gate.

"'Alt! Who goes there?" cried Seaman Lovyer.

The shadow paused, then came the reply "Rounds," briefly.

"Rounds," said the sentry curiously. "What Rounds?"

The suppliant gave a little laugh.

"Visiting Rounds," he said.

"Stand, Rounds, and wait escort," returned Lovyer, whistling for the guard.

In thirty seconds the guard under C.P.O. Chubb was on the scene and passed the visitor through. It was too dark for any of the men to see more than that their charge was wearing a curious Balaclava-like helmet.

Thus they came to the commander.

Ballantyne flashed his light on the visitor for a moment, then:

"Fall out the guard," he said to the C.P.O. abruptly, and a moment after: "What on earth are you doing here at this time of night, Holt?"

"Came to see you," said Holt.

"Nice time for a visit. Should have thought you'd be fairly busy." The commander was not cordial.

"Oh, I've been rather rushed," returned Holt, "but nothing on hand now."

"How d'you get in?"

"I gave 'Visiting Rounds.' They passed me through like a bird."

"You did, did you?" growled the Commander. "It was most irregular."

"Yes," assented Holt, grinning. "The circumstances altogether are most irregular, *most* irregular."

"What d'you want, anyhow?" asked the Commander irritably.

"Three things," said Holt hurriedly, rather nervously. "First to thank you for what you did, licking me into shape, y'know."

"Wouldn't to-morrow have done?" asked Ballantyne ungraciously.

"To-morrow would not have done," said Holt. "To-morrow would never have done." He was quite grave, solemn even.

"And I want to thank you for the way you worked the light just now," he went on.

"Damn condescendin'," said Ballantyne, biting his moustache.

"And last I've come for my fountain-pen."

"What's that!" asked the Commander alertly.

"Come for my fountain-pen, y'know," repeated Holt, grinning joyously.

"Good Lord, man!" Ballantyne broke out. "It was you up there, was it?"

"And other good lads," the airman interjected.

"It was you that brought her down? Well, I'd never have thought it. I'm damn glad you won your bet. Shake hands on it, Holt; shake hands."

He passed the pen across and took Holt's hand; it was clammy cold.

"Where did you come down?" he asked.

"Hanstead," said Holt briefly. Of a sudden the spirit seemed to have gone out of him.

"Easy?"

"No, rotten."

At that moment came the release, and the Commander walked into the office. When he came out again Holt was no longer to be seen.

THE NEXT DAY Ballantyne saw certain news in the paper and, as a consequence, looked up a friend in the motor transport.

"Holt?" said the motor-man. "Yes, I took the body home last night. Dead? Of course he was dead. Dead long before he touched earth. Petrol tank fired, poor chap. Why, a bunch of keys in one of his pockets had fused."

"He was second on my station for a month or two," said Ballantyne rather aimlessly.

There was a moment's silence; the commander wanted to ask a certain question, but felt that he was a fool to do so. Strangely enough it was not necessary.

"Queer thing," said the motor-man abruptly. "He'd got a fountain-pen in his pocket untouched, and they say the stuff's inflammable—untouched. As for the rest of him, he was pretty well a cinder."

"All except his spirit," said Ballantyne.

The motor-man stared at the old sea-dog strangely. "You want a nerve tonic, my son," he said; "that's what you want."

So Commander Ballantyne never told anyone about that fountain-pen.

THE JUNGLE
PAUL EARDLEY

I

A Man of Mystery

WITH A JOY AKIN to that of Adam beholding his first sunrise, Heron stood at the taffrail of the incoming mail-steamer and watched the magic of the dawn as it spread its green suffusion behind the dark line of the Western Ghats, and touched the still waters of the harbour and the waking city of Bombay with glimmering opal fire.

He was bare-headed and blue-eyed, and the breeze of the morning ruffled his crisp, yellow hair till he looked seraphically youthful. Pitching away his cigarette he dug his fists into the pockets of his loose-fitting tussore jacket and drank of that breeze as if he found it the rarest vintage of rapture.

"India at last," he whispered.

Now, India is all things to all men, and because Clive Heron sought her in a spirit of high romance it was romance that she offered unto him. But like Circe or Cleopatra, India mostly tinctures the cup of romance, with strange and ungodly things.

At the shivery hour of three in the morning Heron found himself stretching his cramped limbs on the platform of a small and very drowsy wayside station.

He lit a cigarette and strolled to the other end of the platform. Turning his head presently he saw a shadowy form glide out of the deeper shadows and come to a halt beside his heaped up baggage.

"You are from Mr. Shore?"

The man had salaamed assent as Heron strode up and thereupon assumed the office of guide in the difficult journey up country, which had to be made by means of ponies. For it was to a tea-plantation that Heron was bound, and many of these Assam tea-gardens are somewhat inaccessible places.

The sun was already hot by the time the bungalow came in sight. There was something very homely to Heron in the appearance of that bungalow; it was like a rambling, whitewashed English farmhouse with a thatched roof.

"A consumptive Hercules!" That was Heron's first impression of the man who came stalking down from the veranda to bid him welcome.

Shore, the manager of the tea-garden, was a man of magnificent frame, but sickness or overwork or some other thing had played pathetic havoc with his physique. His garments hung as loosely upon his gaunt figure as the rags on a scarecrow. The head was massive, with handsome, clear-cut features, but his cheeks were painfully hollow and his eyes looked out from cavernous depths with a feverish glitter. In age he might have been anything between thirty-five and fifty.

"Delighted to meet you, Mr. Heron."

It was a deep voice of unmistakable culture. His hand closed over the boy's in a vice-like grip. "Hope you didn't have too much bother getting here? Don't let me keep you here, though," he added, turning on his heel and leading the way to the bungalow. "You're feeling pretty well fagged, I've no doubt. Hope you will get used to our different hours of feeding up here. You'll have time now to have a bath before breakfast." Heron's clothes were sticking to his back.

"Thanks! That's just what I should like!"

"I will put you up for the first few nights while you are getting your things and your place is being put in order. It's a bit out of repair just now."

"Thanks awfully."

Heron sat down to breakfast with about the best appetite he had ever known in his life, but Shore made the merest pretence at eating. He appeared to be thinking deeply.

"You're not married, are you?" he suddenly shot out.

Heron laughed: "Of course not."

"There's a lot of young fellows with wives at home who come out here as single men," said Shore, and his eyes were keen as a hawk's as they met the boy's gaze. "But I won't have any of that sort working for me! If a man has a wife at home and he comes out here and dies, it leads to no end of misery and unpleasantness. My last assistant, for instance—"

"The one who broke his neck?"

"So you've heard about that, have you?" Shore queried sharply.

"I heard in Bombay."

"It was the fellow's own fault," Shore said, in a dry, grating voice. "Any man who is fool enough to go wandering about in the dark on a night when there isn't a moon must expect to get broken bones! But the letters his wife wrote to me—!" He made an expressive gesture. "Why, you might have imagined that I was to blame for his death!"

In spite of the blazing sunlight Heron felt a little shiver creep up his spine. The manager emptied his glass at a draught and refilled it.

"Here!" he said. "Don't let's talk about ghastly things. Try one of these Burma cheroots."

For some time they smoked in silence—a silence punctuated by periodic gurglings from the whisky bottle. Shore was drinking glass after glass of neat spirit.

"You'd better sleep for a couple of hours now," the man said at length, "and then we'll stroll round the tea."

II

THE COOLIE GIRL

THEY WERE A LITTLE LATE in starting. As they made their way along the thread-like paths which wound between the green bushes they met gangs of coolies returning from work with their tools and their laden baskets. Some of the women among them had babies astride their hips, and one who passed close to Shore fingered a string of blue beads round the neck of her child in a curiously nervous fashion.

"What's she doing that for?" asked Heron.

"She thinks I've got the evil-eye, and she's taking precautions in case I should work the child harm. Lots of 'em think I'm accursed!" And he laughed harshly.

And then, the path growing wider, he linked his arm through Heron's and began to talk in the most entertaining fashion. Nor did his genial mood vanish; it continued till dinner that night, increasing in warmth all the time. But as soon as the plates were removed he began to consume whisky as industriously as ever. There was remonstrance in Heron's eyes.

"A man must either sleep or drink," Shore said apologetically. "I can't sleep, so I—do the other thing!"

"But you ought to see a doctor. You'll kill yourself."

Shore puffed out a wreath of smoke. "I wish I'd got the pluck to do that," he said darkly. "But I'm a coward when it comes to death."

Chuckoo-chuckoo-chuck-o-o! came the mysterious mocking cry of a nightjar. A galleon of cloud, slowly sailing through an archipelago of giant stars, heaved to and down from her sank the silver anchor of the waning moon.

Then something stirred in the tea-bushes no more than a dozen yards from the foot of the veranda steps.

"Where on earth did that girl spring from?"

"What girl?" Shore spoke in a thick, faint voice as if he had drawn a cloud of smoke into his lungs and had all he could do to prevent himself choking.

"I say, isn't she a beauty," breathed Heron. "But ought she to be plucking tea at this time of night? Won't she get fever or something?"

"No," answered Shore, still in the same gasping whisper, "she won't—get—fever!"

In the moonlight stood a coolie girl plucking rapidly, all her attention apparently concentrated upon her task. Her face was turned a little from them, but the moonlight seemed to have grown on a sudden much brighter, revealing in all their loveliness the sylphlike lines of her figure. The few wisps of whitish drapery which comprised her garments, emphasised the lissom grace of her contours, and Heron watched her entranced, the man and the artist both fully awake in his blood.

The little twinkling ripple died out of the slim, bronze shoulders. She had ceased from her plucking. For a moment she was motionless, with her arms limp against her sides, and her little palms curled outwards; she seemed very weary. And then her bosom heaved as she drew a long breath, and she stooped.

"She'll never be able to lift that great basket alone!" Heron had sprung to his feet. "I must lend her a hand!"

Shore's fingers closed on his shoulder.

"Sit down!"

Heron turned on him hotly.

"I can't stand by and see her doing such work at this time of night if you can! Let me go!"

Shore glared at him, and then with a throaty chuckle let his hand fall and reached out for the whisky bottle. Heron took two strides forward and reached the edge of the veranda, and then he glanced back. "She's gone!" he breathed in a queer, incredulous voice.

"You must have startled her."

"No, she's vanished; I tell you—disappeared into nothing!"

"Nonsense! The moonlight's misled you. Why, the night is full of shadows!"

Heron sat down again, shaking his head in bewilderment. "I could have sworn—" he began; and then: "But any way what was she doing working at this hour at all?"

"She always comes here to work one night in the year. It's a custom with her."

"You know her, then?"

"Quite well."

"I'm glad of that." He laughed a trifle shakily. "D'ye know, just for a minute I thought she might be a ghost!"

"Fancy your thinking that!" Shore smiled, raising his black, bushy eyebrows. "Here, let's talk of something else! You'll be getting nervous. Tell me about yourself. What part do you come from? You're a public school man, aren't you?"

"I was at Harrow."

"Were you, begad? You—you didn't know a man by the name of Durward?"

"Didn't I, though! Why, little Tony Durward was my special chum."

"And he was fond of you?" said the other hoarsely, his neck craned eagerly forward.

"He was that! The chaps used to call us The Twins."

"Tell me more about him. I'm interested. I used to know his brother."

So Heron gave free rein to his tongue. He was always enthusiastic when he spoke of his chum, and he talked on and on, the distant bray of a stag filling in occasional pauses between his words.

"I think we'd better turn in now," said Shore at last in a weary voice. He rose, stretching himself, and pitched away the stump of his cigar.

"Right you are. But I just want to have another look to see if that girl's about." Heron laughed lightly and walked to the veranda-edge. In the misty moonlight the bamboo-jungle which bounded the tea-garden reared itself like a jagged black cliff against the sky. Not the slightest breath of wind stirred the tea-bushes. Above the spot whence the girl had disappeared a band of fire-flies danced and circled like sparks from an anvil. In the room behind him he could hear the foot-fall of Shore; there was something almost tigerish about it—so heavy and yet so soft.

"Pooh!" said Heron, shaking himself, and walked into the lamp-lit room, whistling through his teeth.

"Well, good-night!" Shore said, and stretched out a large, bony hand.

"Good-night," Heron answered. "I've enjoyed to-day A1."

As Heron made to withdraw his hand Shore flung him back against the table. The lamp met the floor with a crash, blinked and went out. They were wrestling together in the dark.

III

THE CALL

ONLY FOR A MOMENT they struggled; the man had the strength of a giant. Heron felt himself falling—heard his head hit the floor with a thud—and with the paraffin reek in his nostrils he swooned amid the ruins of the lamp.

He opened his eyes painfully. The back of his head felt bruised; he wanted to rub it with his hand. But a rope was cutting into his flesh at a dozen points; he could not move hand or foot; he had been trussed up and fastened to a staple in the wall.

"What's the game, Shore? What's all this foolery?"

Heron could hardly hear himself speak for the singing in his ears.

Shore had lit a candle. He was holding it flame downwards, so that the wax dripped in a little pool upon the table. When the pool was the size of a shilling he placed the base of the candle upon it, pressing it till the candle stood fixed in an upright position. All this he did very methodically.

"What's the game, Shore?" He spoke in a milder voice; if the man were mad he had better humour him. "This rope is cutting my arms most infernally!"

"I'm going to save your life!"

Shore leant across the table, grasping two corners of it with his big, bony hands. "I can't let you go like the others!"

"Who wants my life? I don't understand?"

"You saw that girl in the garden? Well, she's coming to see us to-night."

"What about that?"

"You thought she was a ghost, didn't you?"

Heron nodded.

"Well, *you thought right!*"

A little draught caught the candle, and the shadow of Shore staggered across the room like a drunken Colossus.

"You believe I'm mad? I guessed you would. But I'm telling the truth. I've tied you up to save you from her!"

Heron gazed at him blankly.

"At first I meant to let you go, just as I let my last two assistants, without lifting a hand to save you, but that was before I knew you were Tony Durward's friend. You see, I love little Durward."

"But how do you know him?"

"I am his brother!"

133

A moment of dead silence. Then Shore went on:

"Of course, he never mentioned me to you. He wouldn't. He didn't know you were coming to me. He doesn't even know where I am or what name I'm living under."

He foraged in a pocket of his coat, which had been ripped across the breast in the struggle, and produced a grimy envelope. "Here's the last letter I got from him, poor lad. He said in it that he was going to pray for me every night. For a month that letter was my sheet anchor. It pulled me up and held me fast. And then I broke loose again and drove straight on to the rocks of hell!"

He paused, and brushed his hand across his brow; his face was gleaming with sweat.

"D'ye know, if you hadn't been Tony's chum I'd have sacrificed you, just like the others?"

"Mad"—thought Heron—"stark, staring mad!"

"She was a coolie girl who was working here when I came, and I wanted a mate and took her," he went on feverishly. "I was crazy about her at first. I called her Yasôdhara because she had"—and he quoted softly—"'A form of heavenly mould, a gait like Pavati's, eyes like a hind's in love-time.' And then I got sick of her. Perhaps the whisky was to blame. You see, I'd gone back to it after being off it for a spell, and a man can't love whisky and a woman too. And then—" He broke off, shielding his face with his hand as though to shut out some horror.

"What happened?" breathed Heron, quivering.

"I found her putting something in my drink—caught her in the act—something, she said, to bring back my love and make me adore her always. I was blazing mad for a minute. I snatched up the glass and dashed it in her face. I—blinded her!"

He dropped his hand and stared across at Heron.

"For two days she stayed in the house. I was drunk all the time. And then in the night she went out, and she could not see, and she fell down a *nullah* and died."

Heron sucked in his breath.

"Once a year she comes back," Shore whispered. "She comes for—me. But hitherto she has taken others. I have stood aside and let them go in my place. You see, *she is still blind!*"

134

Heron's brain reeled; he wanted to speak, but his tongue seemed dead at the roots and his mouth seemed filled with sand. The only sound in the room was the ticking of the small silver watch upon his wrist; it had escaped from the struggle uninjured; and in that utter silence its ticking seemed to fill the place.

Then came another sound—a faint, far-off rustling, suggesting the movement of a handful of wind-blown leaves along a gravel path. Shore's jaw dropped. His eyeballs gleamed, white and rolling, and he slid away from the table and flattened himself against the wall in the shadow cast by a bookcase.

Heron strained his ears listening. And then the pain of the ropes which cut torturingly into his flesh left him as suddenly as the pain slips out of a trapped beast's limb when it hears the approach of the hunter.

The soft pit-pat of naked feet was coming up the veranda steps.

Icy paralysis gripped the boy. He had closed his eyes instinctively, in a sudden shrinking of fear, and now he bit his lip hard as a man might do in a desperate effort to awaken from a nightmare. But he felt naught save the tiny spurt of the salt blood into his mouth. The nightmare remained.

There was a rush of cold air upon his forehead, and he knew that the door had been noiselessly opened and shut. Then some power he was helpless to resist caused him to raise his eyelids.

The candle-light glimmered on a slightly clad body and bare, brown limbs. The girl he had seen once already that night was slowly moving towards him.

Her left hand covered her face. Her right was outstretched gropingly before her, the light flickering on a golden bracelet upon the soft, round arm, and twinkling on her little, sharp, red-tinted nails.

Then Heron's heart seemed to stop beating. She had dropped her left hand and was looking at him. No, not looking at him, for her eyes were shut, and right across them ran a ghastly, bluish-white scar.

Her lips were moving. No audible words came from them, but on a sudden as he gazed on the seared face and felt her sinuous, silent approach, a storm of words swept his being. His heart had interpreted the message of her body and lips.

"Back! Get back!" Heron strove to say, but the words stuck in his throat. An uncanny horror possessed him.

Then in a flash the horror passed and his blood leapt and sang in a wild desire for possession. He loved her; she should be his— yes, if it cost him his soul!

She smiled, holding out her arms towards him, and then glided towards the door, where she paused. Heron began to fight frantically with his bonds.

"Wait for me!" he panted. "I'm coming, I—"

Out from the velvet shadow that the bookcase cast crept Shore, his body bent nearly double, his fingers outspread and quivering. There was no passion in his eyes—only fear as he followed the beckoning vision.

The staple gave way at last. Flinging aside the rope that had bound his limbs, Heron staggered out into the night, whither the two had gone. His foot tripped, and he measured his length on the ground. The shock sobered him like a sudden *douche* of cold water. He rubbed his bleeding, earth-stained hands on his thighs. All the erotic madness had cleared from his mind and reins; he felt weak and sick and miserably desolate. Had he walked in his sleep or what? He shivered, then making a megaphone of his hands, shouted:

"Shore, where are you? Shore?"

The tea-bushes rustled mournfully, a faint breeze stirring their leaves. The breeze passed away, and they swayed back into immobility, with a sound suggesting a great congregation rising up from their knees. Then a long-drawn shriek pierced the silence.

Heron's blood froze. He stood rooted to the spot. The shriek was repeated, soaring up in an ear-splitting crescendo, and ending with appalling suddenness.

A narrow path zigzagged away from Heron's feet, the greyish earth gleaming like a snail-track in the rays of the moon. It led to the direction whence the shrieks had come, and Heron moved cautiously along it.

Presently he remembered that he had an electric torch in his pocket. He produced it, and the spear of dancing light that leapt out from it helped his progress. For perhaps ten minutes he walked, calling "Shore! Shore!" at the top of his voice every fifty yards or so. But only vague echoes answered. Presently the earth gleamed no longer under that shaft of brightness.

There was just a black void below it. The path had ended in a precipice.

Lying full length upon the ground, his left hand clutching the stem of a convenient bush, for he was feeling horribly dizzy, Heron probed into the inky depths of the *nullah*. Something white flickered amid a warty growth of thorns some fifty feet down the side. He flashed the lamp more strongly upon it. Part of a man's garment. Shore's?

He rose to his feet, his teeth chattering. Away to the right the descent into the *nullah* was broken by sundry bushes and sloped down at a climbable angle. Worming his way to this point he commenced to move down the treacherous face to the bottom, and at last he stood amid a confusion of jagged boulders, shingle, shrivelled fern, and ankle-deep sand.

Shore was Tony Durward's brother. That was the fact which more than any other drew him forward over the rocks, through the sand, and through briars and weeds toward the spot where the white rag had flickered. The path slanted downwards, and there was a dank smell of mud and slime. Heron stood still. The tip of the flash-lamp beam touched a dim, huddled mass.

"Shore!" he gasped. "Shore, is that you?"

But Shore uttered no reply. He was lying upon his back, with his legs doubled under him, and his eyes staring up at the stars. When Heron sought to raise him his head slid forward with a jerk upon his chest, like the head of a shot wood-pigeon. The expression of that face would have scared a hangman.

"Neck broken!" breathed Heron, retreating. "He must have tripped and—"

He said no more. In the dead man's outflung right hand was clutched a woman's bracelet.

137

THE HAUNTED CHESSMEN
E. R. PUNSHON

I

The Black Queen

IT WAS IN FRED KERR'S ROOMS that I saw them first. For a wonder Kerr was by himself; he was the most popular man I ever knew, I think, and it was the rarest thing in the world to find him alone. But that I had done so this evening rather pleased me, for I was very full of my success against Jenoure Baume, and very anxious to tell Kerr all about it. Even he had never yet beaten Jenoure Baume.

Of course, Baume isn't a master of chess in the sense that are Lasker and Casablanca. Still, for a common or garden player like myself, with a purely local reputation, to beat him is something of an achievement, and I wanted very much to tell Kerr of my success. He was very sympathetic and very interested, and in analysing the game with me he pointed out a move Jenoure Baume might have made which would almost certainly have cost me my queen. Fortunately Baume had not seen it—nor had I for that matter— and I told Kerr he really ought to go in for chess seriously.

"Not enough open air about it for me," he answered laughingly. "I'll take it up when I'm sixty." When I rose to go he mentioned that the date of his wedding had been fixed for the following month.

I congratulated him warmly—Lady Norah was a charming girl, and the match most suitable in every way—and in one of his little confidential outbursts that every one found so charming he told me how happy he was and how fortunate he counted himself.

138

"And is that one of the wedding-presents?" I asked, nodding towards a set of chessmen standing on a board on a small side-table.

I had noticed them as soon as I entered the room. Of Indian workmanship as I guessed, they were very beautifully carved and polished, and when I looked at them again I was conscious of a curious impression. I cannot define it exactly—but it was almost as though they moved and stirred, as though they all watched eagerly, intently. The idle thought came to me that those inanimate carved pieces of polished bone were watching me as a spider from its web watches a fly hovering near.

Vexed with myself for having such foolish fancies—I remember I thought they were due to the strain of my game with Jenoure Baume—I went over to look at them more closely.

"Awfully fine carving!" I said, picking up one of the white pieces. "Indian, isn't it? Are they a wedding-present?

"No," Kerr answered. "The fact is, I bought them from poor Will Lathbury's widow."

"Oh, indeed!" I said.

I had only met Lathbury once or twice, but, of course, I knew him well by reputation as a sound, steady player, and the mysterious tragedy that had ended his life had been a great shock to me.

"Those were the pieces they found near him," Kerr added.

Poor Lathbury had been discovered one morning lying dead across his chessboard on which he had apparently been working out some problem, or analyzing a game. The razor with which he had cut his throat was in his hand, and there was no faintest explanation possible of his miserable deed. It was certainly shown in evidence that for a day or two before the end he had seemed slightly worried, and had spoken about some game of chess or problem that appeared to be troubling him. And he had complained of not sleeping very well, a most unusual thing with him. But that was all. The coroner suggested that his mind had become affected by his intense application to his favourite game, but that was all rubbish. However, the jury returned the usual verdict, and there the matter had to rest.

"Are they ivory?" I asked, looking more closely at the piece I was handling.

"Well, the story goes," answered Kerr, with a touch of hesitation—"the story goes that they are made from human bones."

"Oh, Lord!" I said, putting down a little quickly the piece I was holding.

"I don't know if it's true," Kerr added, "very likely it isn't. It may be just a yarn. But the tale is that an Indian Rajah some time in the Middle Ages captured a hated enemy, killed him, and had these made from his bones."

"Ugh!" I said. "What an idea! What on earth made you get them?"

"I hardly know," he answered. "Mrs. Lathbury wanted to get rid of them—naturally. They hadn't very pleasant associations for her. She asked me what they ought to fetch. I said I would take them if she liked. I thought it was a way to help her, and then it's lovely carving."

"Rather too lovely for me," I said, and I could have sworn that the black queen turned her head and shot at me a glance of malignant and deadly hatred.

Of course, the notion was absurd, and when I looked again I saw the piece as immobile as any other bit of carved bone. And yet when I looked a third time I was once more aware of that air of cruel and furtive waiting as of some evil thing lurking patiently which before had seemed to me to hover over those two double rows of carved figures.

Determined to conquer my fancies I picked up the black queen and, examining it more closely, I thought I made out that it was a trick in the arrangement of the eyes which gave the piece that aspect of alert watchfulness I had noticed.

"Carved out of human bone!" I repeated, weighing the piece in my hand. "What an idea! Well, shall we have a game?"

I thought Kerr looked startled and even a little alarmed. He shook his head quickly without speaking. I felt very relieved; for the idea was powerfully in my mind that it was not against him that I must play, but against some other—some unknown—antagonist.

I said good-night a little hurriedly and took myself off. The fact is, I had wanted to play so badly that I felt that if I stayed there much longer with that black queen in my hand and the pieces drawn up ready, I should find myself making the first move—against Whom, I wondered? Whom or what?

I remember very plainly that as I went out of the room I had a last impression of those pieces drawn up in line as though waiting—waiting with a malign and dreadful patience.

I know my heart was beating faster than usual, and my forehead was a little damp as I came out into the street. The idea was with me that I had escaped some great danger, but what or why I had no idea.

II
A Soul in Torment

A WEEK OR TWO PASSED, and I only remembered my experience of that night to be ashamed of the inexplicable agitation I had felt. Then one day I happened to meet Baume. He knew Kerr fairly well, and declared he was wasting on other pursuits talents that had been meant for chess alone. Then I chanced to mention those curious carved bone chessmen.

"He says they are made of human bone," I remarked, with a laugh. "Gruesome idea, isn't it?"

To my surprise Baume looked very grave. Apparently the old man knew those chessmen well—and did not like them. Finally he blurted out:

"You tell your friend to drop them in the river. That is best for them."

Going home that night I noticed on the placard of one of the evening papers, "Mysterious Suicide," and on that of another, "Strange West End Tragedy." I paid no attention just then, but the next morning over breakfast I noticed a column headed, "Mysterious Death of Well-known Sportsman," and, on glancing at it, I saw that it referred to poor Fred Kerr.

He had been found first thing in the morning lying dead with a bullet through his brain. The pistol with which he had committed the miserable deed was still clasped in his right hand, and the account mentioned that the body lay across a chessboard on which the pieces were arranged in what seemed an unfinished game.

It was a frightful shock to me—indeed it must have been so to all who knew Kerr. I could hardly believe that a man so full of life and spirits, so richly dowered with all good gifts, had ended his life in such a way. There was no explanation. At the inquest a verdict of accidental death was returned, the idea being that Kerr had shot himself while cleaning or examining his pistol.

An attempt was made to suggest foul play on the grounds that the position of the pieces on the chessboard showed that a game had just been concluded, that this game must have been played with someone, and that that someone had disappeared and was, therefore, under suspicion.

Conclusive evidence showed, however, that the unhappy man had been alone all that evening. Of course, the position of the pieces might be accounted for in many ways. He might have been working out an end game, or analysing some position. It was not a problem he had been working on, though, as black was winning and, of course, the problem convention is for white to win.

However, not much attention was paid to the chessmen; and as foul play was ruled out and suicide seemed incredible, the jury fell back on the idea of accident, though there was not the least support for such a theory.

Poor Kerr! I called to leave a wreath and express my sympathy. I asked if I might see my old friend for the last time, and they agreed. With feelings of the utmost sadness I looked my last on my friend's face, and as I did so there came upon me slowly, irresistibly, the idea that he had died in terror and anguish of soul and body.

I felt this impression slowly invade and possess my mind, till I shook and trembled with the knowledge that I stood in the presence of unnameable dread. I began to edge slowly away towards the door, very slowly, for I knew that if I went quickly my panic would overcome me, and I should run, and I knew that would be very dangerous, fatal perhaps. By an intense effort of will I kept my face towards the bed in which lay That which I no longer regarded as the earthly frame of my friend, but felt was changed into something unspeakably horrible and foul. My hair bristled, the flesh crept upon my bones, I forced myself to keep my eyes fixed steadily on the still form upon the bed, though I was sure it was watching me with an intent and evil patience as a spider in its web watches the fly fluttering near—the very sensation I had had before.

Somehow or another, I don't know how, I got to the bottom of the stairs. I stood there, a little dizzy, a little faint, trying to recover myself.

Presently I got out into the street somehow or another, and I know that for some time afterwards I had no liking for the dark and no taste for being alone.

III

THE GATES OF HELL

POOR KERR HAD BEEN THE OWNER of a good many curios he had collected, some of them of value, and when I heard after a time that his friends had decided to sell them at auction, I thought I would go and see if I could pick up some little memento of one I had so much admired and liked.

I bought two rather fine engravings by Meryon; very cheap they were, too. I noticed Mark Norand, the captain of our chess club match team, and after speaking a word or two to him, I was thinking of going when the auctioneer put up the carved bone chessmen.

He did not repeat the tale that they were of human bone—perhaps he thought that wouldn't sound very attractive, or he may not have known the story—but he laid great emphasis on the excellence of the carving. Mark Norand made the first bid, and I know I was very startled. Somehow I hadn't thought of anyone actually buying the things. I said to him:

"I wouldn't have them if I were you."

He looked at me with rather a puzzled and slightly suspicious air.

"Why, do you want them yourself?" he asked.

"Good heavens, no!" I answered, but I could see he did not quite believe me.

In the auction-room everyone is inclined to be suspicious of everyone else. It is a warfare there without quarter and without scruple. Mark Norand was a friend of mine, but he did not mean to be done out of any bargain that was going. He bought the chessmen for three guineas—cheap enough, considering the excellence of the carving.

He was very pleased with himself and his purchase, and his idea that he had got ahead of me. He asked me to go round and play a game with his new possessions. I refused point blank and he laughed. I think he believed I was a little piqued at losing the chessmen.

We got busier than ever at the office, and I was kept very much occupied for some time. I could not even get a spare hour to slip round to the club for a game, and it was quite by accident that I happened to hear some one mention Mark Norand and say that he was looking very ill.

I knew where it was he generally lunched. The place was out of the way for me, and I didn't like the cooking there, but I went the next day. Almost the first man I saw when I entered was Norand. He was sitting at one of the tables with food before him, but he had pushed it away untasted and was pouring over a chess board.

"Hullo, Norand," I said, "working out a problem?"

He looked up at me. I could not help starting. He was greatly altered, but it was not that I noticed so much as the horrid fear I saw peeping out from his bloodshot eyes and lurking in the new lines that had come about his mouth.

"Oh, you?" he said, and to mingle with the fear I read in his eyes there came a fierce dull resentment, so that he looked at me as though he held me for his deadliest enemy.

"You knew, didn't you? Why didn't you tell me?" he demanded.

"Knew what? Tell you what?" I asked.

"Those chessmen," he muttered, shuddering. He added: "Why did you let me buy them?"

"I told you not to; I warned you," I said.

"Told me not to, warned me not to!" he repeated, and gave me a look of deadly hate. "If you saw a man knocking at the gate of

144

hell without knowing it, would you just tell him not to do that and then walk away?"

"Why, what's the matter?" I asked.

He did not answer, and the waiter came up just then. I ordered the first thing I saw on the bill. Norand had become intent on his game again. I noticed it was a position in a game and not a problem he was working at—and the waiter, who knew him as an old customer, and saw I was a friend, observed to me:

"The gentleman's worrying too much over his chess. He hardly eats anything now."

"Has he been long like this?" I asked.

"Only about a week, sir," the man answered.

He brought me what I had ordered, and Norand looked up presently.

"What do you think of this position?" he asked.

"Well, white looks in rather a fix," I answered. "Good Lord, what's the matter?"

I really thought he was going to have a fit; he fell back in his seat, panting for breath and ghastly pale. I might have pronounced his death warrant. I jumped up with some vague idea of getting a doctor but he stopped me.

"No, no, I'm all right," he said—croaked, rather. "For God's sake, look at the board, and see if you can find any way out!"

"For white?" I asked.

"For white," he repeated.

I bent over the board. It seemed to me mate was pretty sure to come in three or four moves. I said:

"Is it a game you're playing?"

He nodded.

"Who's your opponent?" I asked.

He did not answer, and I could see well that a secret and terrible agitation possessed him.

"I don't know," he stammered.

And the idea came to me that he did know but that he dared not say. This seemed to me highly absurd and at the same time quite reasonable.

He wiped his face again.

"You see," he argued, "the thing's impossible."

"I don't know what you mean; I don't know what you are talking about," I said angrily.

But the idea burnt in my mind like fire, that I did know and that I also dared not say.

He leant across the table, his eyes alight with that mingled desperate fear and deadly hate I had seen in them before.

"You ought to have warned me," he muttered. "Mind this, if I lose I will leave you the things in my will."

I remember it did not seem in any way absurd that he should couple together the ideas of losing the game and of making his will.

I was studying the position of the pieces so intently that I, like him, pushed aside my lunch almost untasted. Gradually there was coming back to me a memory of the move poor Kerr had suggested Jenoure Baume might have tried in the game he lost to me. It seemed to me a variation of Kerr's idea might be effective in Norand's present position.

I explained the move. Norand jumped at the idea. We developed it together and, so far as we could see, an attack pressed on those lines was practically sure to win the game. Norand's relief was tremendous, mine scarcely less so. Then all at once his expression changed. He said:

"Suppose when I play the knight it slips of itself on to some other square when I'm not looking?"

I stared at him and laughed. The suggestion seemed so absurd I could not help it.

"Well, of course," I said, "if your pieces do that, I don't see much chance."

He did not answer, and I left the restaurant and went back to the office, feeling relieved in one way, but a good deal worried about poor Norand all the same. His obvious terror, my own odd impressions, all seemed to me fanciful and even ridiculous in the face of his wild suggestion of pieces that moved of their own volition.

All the same I was not surprised when, a day or two later, I heard that the poor fellow had drowned himself in a small pond

146

that lay at the foot of his garden. The account in the papers said he had been sitting up late at chess and that he must have gone straight from the chessboard to his doom.

IV

THE INVISIBLE ANTAGONIST

I COULD NOT HELP making some inquiries about the position of the men on the board. I found, as I had half expected, that they indicated the close of a game in which black had just brought off a mate. My informant told me that presumably poor Norand had been analysing some game. He had not been working out a problem as black was the winning side; and he had not been playing with anyone, as the evidence showed conclusively that he had been alone all the evening.

The usual verdict was returned, and I wrote to Norand's solicitor to say that I absolutely refused to accept any legacy he might have left me.

But I did not post the letter. At one time I had the feeling that the whole thing was pure fancy and that it would be foolish and cowardly to refuse the chessmen if he had really left them to me. And then, again, the idea would come to me that it was all true, but that I was forewarned, and forearmed.

As it happened they were delivered one evening while the Vicar was with me. While he was there I opened the parcel and showed him the chessmen. He was mildly interested and mildly shocked when I told him the tale that they were carved from human bone. He thought it a most repulsive idea, but remarked on the excellence of the carving.

"That black queen, for example," he said, "what an idea of—of—well, vitality, almost, that figure has."

I agreed, and after I had seen the Vicar to the door I went back to my room. I found those chessmen I had left lying on the table where the Vicar had been looking at them, now all drawn up in position on the board.

No living soul, I knew well, had been in the room during my short absence. I stood for a moment or two on the threshold, a little daunted, a little confused, and as I watched I understood that I was expected to play—I saw, too, a thrill of a sinister impatience run through the drawn-up lines of the pieces.

I sat down in front of them. I could not help myself. Each separate piece, from king to pawn, showed animate, palpitating, ready, one and all a-quiver with desire and greed, like hungry beasts of prey waiting for their living victim to be thrown to them. The impression grew in my mind that I was in a more dreadful and more imminent danger than any other living man that night, and that this danger was one that threatened not my life only.

I would have fled, but flight, I knew well, was no longer possible. I tried to mutter a prayer, but the words would not come. I tried to lift my hand to push board and pieces to the ground, but I seemed to have lost control of my arm. The quivering, eager, evil impatience of the pieces increased; I should not have been surprised to see them break into some wild dance of hideous ritual.

All at once they grew quiet, though still instinct with vivid, hungry eagerness, and I felt come upon me a sudden awe and fear and horror as I realised that my Antagonist was there.

I could see nothing, I heard nothing, only I knew well that he was there, that he had come and was seated opposite.

I understood the game was about to begin.

I could not help myself. Slowly I lifted my hand. I swear I did not touch it, but the king's pawn it had been my thought to move slid forward two squares.

A moment's pause and then the black king's pawn, untouched, moved forward in reply. I made my next move, or rather, when I raised my hand with the intention of doing it, the piece transferred itself untouched to the position I had in my mind. The answering move came almost at once. And so the game was played on.

All the time I never touched a piece; once I had made up my mind and raised my hand the piece I was thinking of immediately took up the position I wished. The black pieces did the same; they moved, advanced, retreated, but all in harmony and all in evident obedience to the will of my unseen, unknown Antagonist.

Invisible, but not unknown.

For I was very sure there sat opposite me a man long dead, with an evil face and cruel eyes and hungry, slobbering mouth, wearing the jewelled robes of an Indian prince, and playing with all his skill this game for his master in which the prize was—myself.

I knew that now the game had begun, it had to be finished. I called up all my powers to my aid. I felt my mind grow clear; my nerves were calm and steady. I played my best. I played as I had never played before; I believe I played that night a game that would not have disgraced a master.

More than once I felt I had my Antagonist in difficulties, but each time he retrieved himself. I won a pawn, but lost it again. Still, I began to believe I had a chance of winning.

I pressed hard. I felt a clearness in my brain, a vividness of thought and clearness of vision I have never known before or since. Once or twice, when I was tempted to make a move that might have been dangerous, it was as though I heard a secret whisper warning me to be careful. I knew, too, that my Antagonist was troubled, and I understood that the pieces themselves, both black and white, felt this, and were troubled also.

I had begun a hot attack on the black queen. If I could win her I felt the game would be mine. It was not only that the queen is the most powerful piece, but I realised also that in her lay the focus of the opposing power, that from her or through her there radiated a sort of vigour and encouragement all the other pieces felt—and not the black only but my own white as well.

My attack on the queen failed. I was a move too late, and she slipped out of the net I had so nearly drawn around her. The failure left my position less strong, and I found myself attacked in my turn. I rallied my forces, but the pressure grew stronger and stronger.

The critical point was on my left, where I was beginning to plan a counter-attack. It promised well, and I was beginning to make progress when I found a return thrust aimed at me.

I was puzzled, and, on looking, found that the position of my pieces was no longer as it had been, but a much weaker one. I could not understand, for I was sure I had not moved them. As I looked and wondered I was aware that my unseen Antagonist smiled evilly to himself, and the black queen shook with a horrid, secret merriment that spread and spread till every piece upon the board, black and white, was laughing wickedly to itself, rejoicing in the prospect of my defeat.

I realised in a flash that one of my pawns had turned traitor and, when I was not looking, had slipped back from the square where I had placed it to the one behind where it was so much less effective.

V

AT THE ELEVENTH HOUR

IT COST ME MY BISHOP before I could re-establish my position, and the small inner voice I had seemed to hear before whispered to me that I must watch closely and unceasingly, or the same thing would happen again. I understood that my Antagonist, smiling evilly to himself, could make any one of my pieces betray me, and that this foul play he kept ever in reserve to help him at need. No wonder that he had always won his games all through the centuries!

I was a piece to the bad now, and I had the double strain of playing and of watching to see that none of my men slipped from the squares on which I had placed them. I set my teeth and played my best. I lost another piece, and my king, hotly attacked, was pinned into one corner. Still I fought on, though my brow was wet and my hands shook, and upon me lay the consciousness of impending doom.

I made one last feeble attempt at a counterattack. I do not think it could possibly have saved me, but it was audacious, a little disconcerting, and meant delay at the least. And that was something, for I knew that if I could hold out till cock-crow I should earn at least a day's respite. That my Antagonist knew also, and he grew, one must suppose, impatient.

I was watching my pieces intently since there was not one of them but would have played the traitor had chance offered. My new attack hinged on the one rook I had remaining, and suddenly I saw it sliding away from where it stood to an adjoining square, where it would have been comparatively useless. It stopped when my eye fell on it, for apparently they had no power to move—or my Antagonist no power to make them move—when I was watching, and then something made me look away again. Instantly the rook slipped off to the adjoining square, and at once again all the other pieces, black and white alike, shook with a passion of secret, evil laughter.

For a moment despair overcame me, for now it was only a question of mate in two moves.

But, as before a tiny voice had whispered to me to be cautious when I had contemplated an unsound move, so now again I heard that small, still voice sound clear and vivid in my ear. I knew that my one hope was to do as it advised.

I sprang to my feet.

Pointing at the rook that had moved I cried with a loud voice: "I appeal."

I was aware of an instant, fierce commotion all around me; I saw the pieces, black and white, all palpitant; I heard no sound, but I knew that my Antagonist was dismayed and troubled.

Again I cried:

"I appeal."

The fierce tumult and commotion I was aware of all round, grew yet wilder and more fierce. Though I heard nothing, saw nothing, I knew that all about was fury, dismay, excitement, a hurrying to and fro of strange and evil things, a passage of vast and awful shadows. The pieces were all quivering with hatred and alarm. My dread, long dead Antagonist seemed to me to be screaming hoarsely in an agony of protest and pain. Though still I heard, saw, felt nothing, I was somehow conscious that I stood in the very centre of a chaos of invisible, conflicting powers; that unimaginable forces were aimed against me, but that nevertheless I stood protected. For the third time I cried out very loudly:

"I appeal."

That strange and awful tumult passed. All was still and silent, all that had filled my small room so dreadfully fled swiftly far away. The chessmen were no longer animate and palpitant, but were quiet as any other bits of carved bone; I had a vision of my Antagonist, baffled, howling, far in the depths of nethermost space.

I knew I was safe now, and I knew also what next I had to do. The still, small voice I had heard before had whispered that to me also, and I hurried to obey. I swept the chessmen into their box, and carrying it carefully in my hands, I went into the garden, out by the side gate, and up the lane that leads to the churchyard.

Dawn was grey in the east, the cocks were crowing as I reached it. There amidst the graves, in earth consecrated by holy words for the last resting-place of men, I dug with my bare hands and buried deep the box and the pieces of carved bone it held, deep in the shadow of a cross reared on a grave near by. There I left them to rest for ever; and so, drunk with weariness and terror, went back to my home to rest in peace and thankfulness and safety.

THE EIGHTH LAMP
ROY VICKERS

I

ON THE UNDERGROUND

WITH A MUFFLED, METALLIC ROAR the twelve-forty-five, the last train on the Underground, lurched into Cheyne Road Station. A small party of belated theatre-goers alighted; the sleepy guard blew his whistle, and the train rumbled on its way to the outlying suburbs.

A couple of minutes later, Signalman George Raoul emerged from the tunnel, swung himself on to the up-platform and switched off the nearest lamp. Simultaneously a door in the wall on the down-side opened and the stationmaster appeared.

"Nothing to report, Mr. Jenkins," said Raoul. He spoke in an ordinary speaking voice, but in the dead silence of the station his words carried easily across the rails—words that were totally untrue. He had something of considerable importance to report, but he knew that if he were to make that report he would probably he marked down as unfit for night duty, and he could not afford to risk that at present.

"All right, George. Good-night."

"G'night, Mr. Jenkins."

Raoul passed down the length of the up-platform, dousing each light as he came to the switch. Then he dropped on to the track, crossed and made for the farthest switch on the down-platform.

Cheyne Road Station was wholly underground—it was but an enlarged strip of tunnel—and the lighting regulations did not apply to it. There were eight lamps on each platform.

153

The snap of the switch echoed in the deserted station like the crack of a pistol. Raoul started. The silence that followed gripped him. Pulling himself together he hurried on to the second switch.

"*Ugh!*"

By the third lamp he stopped and shuddered as his eye fell upon a recruiting poster. In the gloom the colouring of the poster was lost—some crudity in the printing asserted itself—and the beckoning smile of a young soldier seemed like the mirthless grin of a death mask. And the death mask was just like—

"You're all right," he assured himself aloud. "It's the new station that's doing it."

Yes, it was the new station that was doing it. But he would not grumble on that account. It was a bit of rare luck, being transferred from Baker Street—just when he was transferred. For all its familiarity, he could never have stood night-work at Baker Street—now.

Even after three weeks in the new signal-box he could never "pass" a Circle train without a faint shudder. The Circle trains had a morbid fascination for him. They passed you on the down-line. Half a dozen stations and they would be pulling up at Baker Street. Then on through the tunnel and, in about an hour, back they came past your box and still on the down-line. In the Circle trains his half-nurtured imagination saw something ruthless and inevitable—something vaguely connected with fate and eternity and things like that.

His mind had momentarily wandered so that he took the fourth switch unconsciously. As he made for the fifth, his nerve again faltered.

"Didn't ought to have taken on this extra work," he seemed to shout into the dark mouth of the tunnel.

"'Tain't worth it for three bob. It's the cleaner's job by rights."

Yes, it was the cleaner's job by rights. But the cleaner was an old man, unreliable for night-work and when the station-master had offered Raoul the job of "clearing up last thing" for three shillings a week, he had jumped at it. The three shillings would make life perceptibly brighter for Jinny—her new life with him.

Between the fifth lamp and the sixth was the stationmaster's den. On a nail outside the door hung the keys with which Raoul would presently lock the ticket-barrier and the outer door of the booking-office.

He snatched the keys as he passed and then, as if to humanise the desolation, he broke into a piercing, tuneless whistle that carried him to the seventh lamp.

A trifling mechanical difficulty with the seventh switch was enough to check the whistling. For a moment he stood motionless in the silence—the silence that seemed to come out of the tunnel like a dank mist and envelop him. He measured the distance to the switch of the eighth lamp. The switch of the eighth lamp was by the foot of the staircase. He need scarcely stop as he turned it— and then he would let himself take the staircase two, three, four steps at a time.

Click!

The eighth lamp was extinguished. From the ticket-office on the street level a single ray of light made blacker the darkness of the station. But Raoul, within a couple of feet of the staircase, waited, crouching.

His hand clutched the stair-rail and he twisted his body round so that he could look up the line. He could not see more than a few feet in front of him, but he could hear, distinct and unmistakable, the rumbling murmur of an approaching train.

All his instincts as a railway man told him that his senses were deceiving him. The twelve-forty-five was the last train down—and he and the stationmaster had together seen it through. There were a dozen reasons why it would be impossible for another train to run without previous notification to the signalling staff. And yet— the rumbling was growing momentarily louder. The air, driven through the tunnel before the advancing train, was blowing like a breeze upon his face.

Louder and louder grew the rumbling until it rose to the familiar roar. In another second he would see the lights.

But there were no lights. The train lurched and clattered through the station and was swallowed up in the down-side tunnel. There were no lights, but Raoul had seen that it was a Circle train.

II

The Doubt

For a nightmare eternity he seemed to be rushing with gigantic strides up an endless staircase—across a vast hall that had once been a ticket-office, and then:

"Hi! Where yer comin' to?"

The raucous indignation of the night constable, into whom he had cannoned, recalled him to sanity.

"Sorry, mate!" he panted. "I didn't see you—as I come by."

"Call that comin' by?" demanded the constable. "Why, you was running like a house afire! What's going on down there, then?"

"Nothing," retorted Raoul.

The constable, unsatisfied, walked through the ticket-office and peered over the barrier. The silence and the darkness gave him a hint.

"Bit lonesome down there, last thing, ain't it?" he suggested.

"Yes," grunted Raoul, as he locked the barrier, "somethin' chronic."

"I know," said the constable. He had not been on night duty for ten years without learning the meaning of nerves.

A short chat with the constable served to restore Raoul's balance, after which he locked up as usual and made his way to the tenement he shared with Jinny, resolving that this time he would report the occurrence to the stationmaster on the following day.

During their three weeks' occupation of the tenement Jinny had made a practice of waiting up to give him his supper. As he came in she was lying asleep, half-dressed, in the second-hand upholstered armchair that had been theirs for three weeks.

"Hullo, Jinny!" he called, with intentional loudness. He wanted to wake her up thoroughly so that she would chatter to him.

"Blessed if I hadn't dropped off!" she exclaimed by way of apology, as she hastily got up and busied herself with his cocoa.

"There's no need for you to wait up, you know, Jinny," he said, as he seated himself at the table. "Only I'm not denying as I'm glad to see you a bit before we turn in."

"Funny thing 'appened to-night," he went on. "After I'd seen the twelve-forty-five through and Mr. Jenkin's 'ad gone and I'd nearly finished turnin' off the lights—"

He told the whole story jovially, jauntily, as if it were a rather good joke. He attained a certain vividness of expression which only became blurred at that part which dealt with his own sensations after the passing of the train.

The woman was wide awake before he had finished. All her life she had indirectly depended on the Underground Railway, and knew its workings almost as well as the signalman himself.

"'Arf a mo', George!" she said, as he finished. "How did it get past the signal if you was out of your box?"

"That's what beats me!" exclaimed George Raoul, thumping the table as if herein lay the very cream of the joke.

She looked at him with the dawning suspicion that he had been drinking; but as she looked she knew that he had not.

"What sort o' train was it?" she asked, keeping her eyes fixed on his.

For a moment he did not reply. His gaze dwelt on his cocoa as he answered:

"Circle train."

Jinny made no reply, and the subject was dropped.

An hour later neither of them was asleep.

"Jinny," said Raoul, "what yer thinkin about?"

"Nothing," she retorted, and her voice came sulkily through the darkness.

"Go on. Out with it!"

"All right! 'Ave it your own way, an' don't blame me. I was wonderin' what Pete was doin' now—this minute."

"Pete!" echoed Raoul, through teeth that chattered, though he tried to clench them. "You've no call to wonder about 'im—not after the way he served you, his lawful, wedded wife."

"I didn't mean to," she defended herself; "only you tellin' me about that train—and 'im being a Circle driver—set me off."

157

"You've no call to think about 'im," repeated Raoul doggedly. "You can lay he ain't thinkin' about you—'e's thinkin' about the woman he left you for."

There was a moment's silence, and then:

"P'r'aps—and p'r'aps not," replied Jinny.

III

THE OFFER OF SILENCE

ON THE FOLLOWING MORNING Raoul decided that he would still say nothing to the stationmaster about the train that had followed the twelve-forty-five.

The position was by no means an easy one. He knew that his nerves would not stand the strain of turning out the lights on the platform—not yet awhile, anyhow. On the other hand, he dared not throw up his job. During the last three weeks he had seen something of Jinny's nature; and although his animal love for her had in no way abated, he had a pretty shrewd suspicion that she would not face even temporary destitution with him.

After much deliberation, he hit on a comparatively neat compromise. As he left home to go on duty he approached an elderly loafer leaning against the wall of a public-house near the station.

"Suppose you don't want a tanner a night for five minutes' work as a child could do?" he suggested.

"All accordin' to what the work is," answered the loafer.

"Turnin' off the lights mostly," said Raoul. "Anyway, if you want the job 'ang about 'ere"—indicating the station—"at twelve-forty-five sharp until you see the stationmaster come off. Then 'op into the station. You'll find me on the platform."

"I'm doing this on me own," he added. "My missis likes me to be 'ome early, and it's worth a tanner a night for a bit of 'elp. See?"

The loss of the extra three shillings a week, Raoul decided, could safely be ascribed to an act of war economy on the part of the railway company. Better lose three bob a week than have to chuck up your job, he reasoned.

The services of the loafer proved a wise investment. Raoul showed him where to find the switches. On the first night he explained it

158

all over and over again, glancing from time to time towards the tunnel, thereby extracting full value for his sixpence.

The explanation finished, and while three lamps remained burning, he left the loafer for a suddenly remembered duty on the ticket-office level. Thence, in a comfortable circle of light, he presently called:

"Turn off them last three lights, mate, and come up."

The loafer sluggishly obeyed, and then shambled up the staircase to receive the most easily earned sixpence of his life.

"Same time to-morrer night if you're on," said Raoul.

"I'm on right enough," replied the loafer.

That formula was repeated every night for some half-a-dozen nights. Then came a night on which the loafer failed to appear.

For five minutes Raoul waited. He went up to the street level and looked round. The station was deserted—there was not even a constable on point duty.

When the loafer's defection became obvious, Raoul's first thought was to leave the lights burning and go straight home. Reflection showed that this would mean the sack—which in turn would mean the probable loss of Jinny—the loss of that for which the very agonies he was now enduring had been incurred.

Besides, there was another thought that drove him back into the station. Somehow or other he would be compelled to explain why he had left the lights burning—why he had been afraid to return to the station. They would ask questions. And God knew where those questions might lead!

The up-platform presented no terrors. On the down-platform— in the moment of utter darkness when the eighth lamp was extinguished—he knew that his fear would reach its zenith. And precisely at that moment the distant rumbling in the tunnel began— the driven air, like a breeze, played about his temples.

He could not prevent his eyes from staring in the direction of the tunnel. He tried to move backwards up the staircase, but all power of voluntary action had left him.

The train seemed to slacken speed as it rolled into the station. As it came towards him, slowly and more slowly, his eyes were glued

159

to a faint luminosity in the driver's window—a luminosity that gathered shape as it came nearer and nearer.

"*Pete!*" he gasped—and with that conscious effort of the muscles his brain regained control of his body and he rushed up the stairs, uncertain whether the train had stopped—knowing that if it came again it would stop and wait for him.

Jinny was awake and moving about the room when he returned. She glanced at his drawn face and knew what had happened.

"Seen it again?" she asked.

"Wot if I have?" he demanded.

"Nothing," she retorted.

She waited while he ate his supper in silence.

"George," she said, as he put down his cup for the last time.

"Well?"

"Suppose we knew for certain as Pete was dead"—she paused, but did not know enough to look at his mouth, and his eyes were turned from her—"why, then we—we could get spliced proper, couldn't we?"

Still avoiding her gaze he nodded.

"Suppose," she said, leaning across the table until her elbows touched his, "suppose we was to go about the banns to-morrer?"

Then did Raoul look up and meet the woman's gaze. In her eye there was nothing of accusation. But there was nothing of doubt.

"Right-o!" he said.

IV

The Tower of Strength

ON THE FOLLOWING MORNING they went together to the parish church and, being recommended thence to the vicarage, explained their needs. They learnt that they would have to wait for three Sundays before they could be married.

He was gloomy and depressed as they left the vicarage.

"Three weeks'll soon pass," she said, as if to console him.

"Aye," he grunted.

"An' you'll feel a lot better when it's done," she added.

To this he made no reply, and she did not labour the point. Indeed, it was the last veiled allusion she ever made to the subject.

160

On his way to the station he came across the loafer in the usual place outside the public-house. The man shambled towards him ready with an excuse, but Raoul cut him short.

"Shan't be wantin' you no more," he said gruffly, and thereby burnt his boats behind him.

During the hours that passed between his going on duty in the early afternoon and his leaving the box after the passing of the twelve-forty-five, he did not once repent having dispensed with the services of the loafer. True, his mind dwelt almost continuously on the ordeal before him. But Jinny had unconsciously given him a weapon when she had told him he would feel better when *it* was done.

That night, as he doused the eighth lamp, he turned and faced the tunnel.

"I'm actin' square by 'er now, ain't I?" he shouted.

Then, for all the furious beating of his heart, he walked at a leisurely pace up the staircase, and so, completing his duties, into the street.

On the next night it was easier, and, with each night that brought his marriage nearer, his confidence grew. His nerve would falter sometimes, but always he managed to ascend the staircase one step at a time. Jinny was a secret tower of strength to him—so that all went reasonably well with him until, by the merest accident, the tower of strength crumbled.

Three Sundays had passed since their visit to the vicarage when the accident happened. The accident took the form of his meeting Mabel Owen as he was returning home from duty.

He had known Mabel in the Baker Street days before he had known Jinny—a fact of which Jinny was well aware. Mabel was returning from some unmentioned errand in the West End when she ran into him and exclaimed:

"Blessed if it ain't George Raoul! 'Ow goes it, George? Seems ages since we met, don't it! An' what might you be doin' in these parts?"

"I work over 'ere now," explained Raoul. "Cheyne Road. 'Ow goes it with you?"

Then, because he had no wish to appear churlish to a girl with whom he had once walked out, he invited her to an adjacent coffee stall. He arrived at the tenement barely half an hour later than usual. But that half-hour was more than enough for Jinny.

"You're late, George," she said, as he came in.

"Sorry, Jinny," he replied. "Couldn't help meself. Met a friend as I was comin' off. Had to say a civil word to 'er."

"*'Er!*" repeated Jinny.

"Mabel Owen," he said—and his clumsy effort to say it casually fanned her suspicion.

"Oh!" shrilled Jinny. "So you keep me waitin' while you go gallivantin' about with that dressed up bit o' damaged goods!"

"You've no right to say that of Mabel," protested Raoul.

"No right!" she echoed. "Oh, no! I've no right to say that of 'er, me livin' with you with no weddin'-ring as you've given me. No better than 'er, I'm not. And don't you let me forget it neither, George Raoul!"

"Stow that, Jinny!" he commanded, with rising anger. "Ain't we fixed it up to get spliced proper day after to-morrer?"

The glint in his eye, partly of anger but partly also of fear, restrained her from further outburst and drove her indignation inwards so that she sulked.

She was still sulking on the following day, compelling him to eat his midday meal in gloomy silence, wherefore he left home for work sooner than was necessary.

V

THE RUMBLING HORROR

HE WAS IN THE SIGNAL-BOX before he recognised that the secret tower of strength had crumbled as a result of the accident of his meeting with Mabel Owen. Jinny had shown him a side of her nature that had been conspicuously absent in the earlier stages of his infatuation. And now his life was to become irrevocably linked with hers.

With the first taste of the bitterness of his sin came remorse; and with remorse came, with renewed strength, the terror which he had partly beaten back. The terror began to grip him even before the stationmaster had left. In the signal-box he had formed

162

the plan of telling the stationmaster that he could not turn out the lights that night—that he must hurry to the bedside of a dying child—any lie would do provided it saved him for that night. To-morrow night he would be married to Jinny. He would have made what reparation lay in his power and would feel the safer.

"Good-night, George."

"G'night, Mr. Jenkins."

The stationmaster hung the keys on the nail outside his den and walked off. Raoul would have called after him, but checked himself. The stationmaster would not believe that lie about the dying child. His face would betray his terror—his terror of the tunnel. The stationmaster would ask him why he was afraid of the tunnel, and—*God knew where those questions would lead!*

"Funny it's wors'n ever to-night!" he said, as he finished the lights on the up-platform—for he was not analytical and did not wholly understand why the secret tower of strength had crumbled. He only knew that he did not want to marry Jinny on the following day. He only saw his sin in gaining possession of her—in the way that he had gained possession of her—in its naked hideousness.

The odd fatalism of his class prevented him from shirking the lights on the down-platform. What has to be will be. The same fatalism drove him ultimately to dousing the eighth lamp and turning, like a doomed rat, to face the already rumbling horror of the tunnel.

More slowly than before, as if it knew that he must wait for it, the train came on. Then in his ears sounded the familiar grinding of the brakes. The train had stopped in the station. The faint luminosity in the driver's window grinned its welcome. Then it beckoned.

"I'm comin', Pete."

From the corner by the staircase, where he had been crouching, he moved across the platform and boarded the train.

VI

A WOMAN SPURNED

Dawn, breaking over the serried roofs of Chelsea, found Jinny sitting wide-eyed before the untouched meal she had prepared hours ago for Raoul.

As if the first faint streaks of light ended her vigil she dropped her face on her arms and burst into tears.

"Fool that I was! Why couldn't I 'ave 'eld me jore about Mabel Owen till we was spliced proper? And now he's left me, and Pete—"

The passion of weeping rose to its height, spent itself, and left her in another mood.

"'E needn't think 'e can get away as easy as all that," she muttered savagely. "If I'm a fool, he's a worse one—as 'e'll soon find to 'is cost."

At eight o'clock she washed herself and donned her black dress. Thus arrayed as a respectable woman of the working-class she made her way to the nearest police-station and asked for the Inspector.

"I'm Mrs. Pete Comber," she explained. "My husband used to be a driver on the Underground. Circle train, he druv."

"Well?" said the Inspector.

She did not hesitate in her confession. She had weighed the cost of her revenge, and did not shrink from paying it.

"A man called George Raoul used to lodge with us—a signaller, 'e was, and worked at Baker Street. Me and 'im got friendly, if you understand, only I wouldn't 'ave nothing to do with him while I was livin' with my 'usband, not being that sort.

"'Bout a couple of months ago George come to me and says, 'Jinny,' he says, 'you won't see Pete no more,' he says. 'Why not,' I says. 'Cos he's gone off with Carrie Page,' he says. 'Chucked up his job and everythink,' he says; 'met him when we was bein' paid,' he says, 'an' he asked me to tell you quite friendly like,' he says."

"Look here," interrupted the Inspector, "we can't have anything to do with all this."

"You wait," replied Jinny, scarcely noticing the interruption. "As soon as George told me, I was that wild with my 'usbin that I let George take me off—me that had always been a respectable woman. Never entered my 'ead as he wasn't tellin' the truth. Next day George was turned on to Cheyne Road an' we come to live up 'ere.

"Well, first he begun tellin' me as he'd bin seein' things on the Underground. That started me thinkin'. I can put two an' two together, same as anyone else, an' I started takin' notice of what he was talking about in 'is sleep. And I tell you as sure as I stand here, George Raoul killed my 'usbin, and I dessay 'e's put 'im in one of the old holes in the Baker Street tunnel wot they used to use for storin' the tools."

The Inspector began to take notes and to ask a number of questions. Of one thing only was he sure—that the woman before him was giving a genuine expression of opinion.

"And now George has left you, I suppose, and that's why you've come along to us?" he suggested.

"He has left me," replied the woman. "But I only found all this out properly night before last, an' I couldn't be sure. I'd have come along 'ere any'ow."

The Inspector guessed that the last statement was a lie. But unless the man, when they caught him, definitely implicated the woman he knew that the Crown would not prosecute her.

"All right," he said. "We'll find George for you. Leave your address and call here to-morrow."

The Inspector, after instructing a plain-clothes man to shadow Jinny to her home, went to interview the Cheyne Road station-master.

On the following morning, when Jinny called at the police-station, she was asked to examine a suit of clothing, a pocket-knife, and a greasy case containing a number of small personal papers and other belongings.

"Yes, they're Pete's right enough, pore dear!" she exclaimed, and then burst into a flood of maudlin tears.

The Inspector waited unmoved. He believed not at all in the genuineness of Jinny's grief; but convention had its claims, and he said nothing until the storm of tears had subsided.

"Now, Mrs. Comber," he said presently, "I want you to dry your face and come along o' me.

"It's all right," he added. "Nothing's going to happen to you."

He took her for some distance in a taxi-cab to a low, vault-like building near the river. There, after parley with the local officials, he led her to an inner room.

165

"Steady now," he warned her. "We're going to show you a dead body."

Some one removed a cloth, and at the same moment, the Inspector demanded:

"Who's that?"

"George Raoul!" gasped Jinny.

As the Inspector, taking her by the arm, led her from the room a question forced itself to her lips. "You—you ain't 'ung him already?"

"No," replied the Inspector, with a grim laugh, "we ain't 'ung him. Wasn't needed. We found your husband in that disused hole, same as you said—and we found George Raoul alongside him—like that. Heart failure, the doctor says. Funny thing! As far as I can make out, he must have been skeered or something and run all the way through the tunnel from Cheyne Road to Baker Street where he done it. Must have been the running as did for his heart."

That, at any rate, was the explanation based on the findings of the Coroner's Court.

BILL DIXON STANDS BY

J. CHAPMAN ANDREWS

I

The Fortune of War

U. 502 WAS THE PRIDE OF BREMEN. When she came in from a cruise folk hung out flags and the Burgomaster invited Commander Max Fielder to luncheon, where there were speeches, many "Hoch, hochs!" and much sweet champagne.

That was over a year ago. In the meantime U. 502 had been baptised and re-christened of a more glorious fellowship. The baptism had been a long ceremony and one which I am not at liberty to reveal. One circumstance marred the complete perfection of the work. When U. 502 was constrained by divers to leave the mud on which she had lain for a week and had been escorted ceremoniously by two tugs and three destroyers into Nidport, she was persuaded to give up her dead: Max, the darling of Bremen, sixteen seamen of the German Navy, and an officer of the British Mercantile Marine.

This last was Bill Dixon, Captain William Dixon of the S.S. *Utopia*, owned by the Blue Triangle Line. Everyone in shipping knew Bill, and a very large circle mourned his death when the *Utopia* appeared under "Boats Sunk" in the evening papers. The pluck and the sea-knowledge of the man, his whole-hearted hatred of the thugs of the sea, had earned him a great reputation. How he had been saved no one could tell, but the irony of his death at the hands of his own countrymen on a German submarine added poignancy to the tragedy.

However, U. 502 was duly swept and garnished and reappeared one fine autumn morning in a new coat of slate grey, a couple of new plates in her bows, her new title, U.C. 07, on her conning-tower and a new old flag on her flag-staff—the White Ensign. So she went forth on the very secret, importunate occasions for which she and her sisters use the undersea.

It is well understood that she had finally washed off the gross acquaintance of the darling of Bremen. She had quickly found a new love, Stanton Towers, Lieut., R.N. Towers was a middle-aged, old-man boy of twenty-five; that is to say, he had the steady nerve of the first period, the prudent sagacity of the second, and the merry daring of the last. He could teach professors the higher mathematics of the lower seas, hold with confidence and full realisation the lives of a dozen honest seamen in his hand unperturbed, and make himself the merry centre of a kids' Christmas party with equal facility. They make them like that at Dartmouth.

There was, however, one corner of U.C. 07 where the paintbrush had stopped short. It was the captain's state-room. In the wicked old days the state-room had been given up by the darling of Bremen to the housing of captive captains and, for the four days between the sinking of the *Utopia* and the accident which led to the redemption of U. 502, Bill Dixon had occupied it. What thoughts he had, plucked from the sea when his whole ship's company went down, no man may say, nor how he bore himself among that fiend fellowship where fate had cast him; but one mark he left of his tenancy. On the enamelled plating of the room he had scratched two lines of verse:

"I'm sorry for Mr. Bluebeard:
    I'm sorry to cause him pain:
But—"
    W.D." (Then came the date.)

Towers had looked over his new command while painting was in progress. He had seen the lines and ordered them to be left. Most people in the service could have named the author and understood.

168

At any rate, Towers did. He saw why Bill had chosen something cryptic; a Shakespeare reference would have been easy reading to a German. The Teuton psychology cannot grasp Kipling.

"You'll never fill in your 'but,' old man," said Towers thoughtfully, "but I may help. We'll let it stay."

In a curious way the lines got hold of him. Into his brain; his throbbing engines went to the tune of it.

> "We're sorry for Mr. Bluebeard:
>   We're sorry to cause him pain:
> But a terrible spree there's sure to be
>   When he comes here again."

He knew that Bill Dixon had Max and the whole *personnel* of the Imperial Navy in mind under that most disrespectful nickname.

II

AN UNKNOWN QUANTITY

IN DUE TIME U.C. 07 went out on her trials, which she endured patiently and with credit, and received the wages of going on. She was given her fill of fireworks and oil, a gramophone with records for all occasions (from the Bishop of London to George Robey), a large complement of woollies, and a kitten. Thus equipped, she crept out one night into the grey seaways entirely unchaperoned and laid a course for three days over shoals and through tide-ripped deeps till she came up at last with a captivating bonnet of drift ice beside a low island in a sea dressed in mud-banks and blue mist. Thereafter she lay secretly down on the mud in the daytime and slunk furtively across the seas after dark, while Towers and his men strove to keep warm.

That was the time that George Robey and the Bishop of London came in useful. (The perspicuous reader will have noticed that submarine conditions demand a varied order of precedence.) The men crawled sluggishly about while Findlay, Engineer-Lieut., did wonderful things to keep his engines from freezing. Of course, in these days they were mostly on top, where the crew could keep their blood in circulation by exercise on the fifty-foot, ice-covered deck. Stanton Towers found the lady somewhat fickle in the circumstances. She packed up drift ice on her nose until it altered all her diving angles, while every time she came up the periscope froze over and left her blind. Then the hatches froze; when open they would not close, and when closed they refused to open.

To add to the catalogue a weird spirit got about the ship. No one could account for it; no one could define it even, but there it was. There were little bits of evidence which one could only laugh at in judicial moments, nothing tangible.

Mainly it was the "someone standing beside you" feeling, which is curious in a submarine, where from the officers' mess you can put your right hand on the galley stove and your left on the engine-room controls. There was a failure of the lights once, which left fourteen men abjectly cursing in the varied argots of Whitechapel, Sauciehall Street, Tyneside, Devonport and Osborne.

As a matter of fact the occasion was trying. U.C. 07, with her periscope flirting with the wave-tops, had spotted smoke on the horizon. They were only thirty-six hours out at the time and still in open sea. Towers received the report, and, though strange smoke was not specifically mentioned on his orders, he decided to proceed as requisite. A certain latitude is granted mariners of the underseas.

U.C. 07 bobbed up tentatively a few minutes later and conned the stranger. Towers had taken command. He called up Calthrop, his second, and took him into council.

"What d'ye make of her, Mabel?"

Calthrop had a complexion that won for him a nickname and much feminine admiration, both of which he loathed.

"She's nothing British on God's earth," said Mabel.

"And so say all of us," returned the owner, and ordered: "No. 1 torpedo tube, ready."

Now, as a matter of fact, both Towers and Calthrop were in error, though they need not be blamed. The mysterious stranger, carrying twelve hundred men and two million pounds in steel to her doom was a changeling child. She had been built on the Tyne to the specifications of the Government of—Moravia, let us say. Moravia—let us say—built and was not able to finish, therefore the

170

hulk had remained the standing joke of Tyneside till the Sultan of Morocco—or any other old place—had bought her up as a bargain to lay the foundations of his navy. She was on the point of completion when war broke out, and had accordingly been seized by order from Whitehall, while Morocco had to be content with mere hard cash instead of cold steel. It may be guessed that she was a monster, for Moravia followed the Admiralty designs of Berlin, while Morocco added a liberal flavour of Saharan architecture.

Towers and Calthrop recognised Germany in her shape and weight. Her very location was suspicious, and, though they saw no flag, there was no doubt in their minds that she was an enemy, and down she should go. So they edged nearer, for a drift of sea fog was coming down, and Towers made his calculations and shifted the helm over.

It was, maybe, two seconds before he would send the order to No. 1 tube to shut down. His hand was on the signal lever when, on a sudden, the lights failed. The whole ship was in darkness except the table where the periscope threw its panorama of the sea above. That was plainer than ever.

"Lights," yelled Towers to the engines. "Oh, you blighted greasers, lights!"

There was the patter of feet up the steps into the conning-tower and an A.B.'s head rose into the grey circle of light spilt from the table.

"No. 1 tube reports light failure, sir, and waits orders."

"Stand fast to carry on," said Towers curtly.

Findlay's voice came through its appointed tube. "Cannot account for failure. Auxiliaries at work in thairrty seconds."

"Very good, carry on," said the owner, but he knew that thirty seconds would have spoilt his present chance, though another might present itself.

In twenty-seven seconds by Findlay's watch the miracle was accomplished, and the crew at No. 1 tube sprang to position again like leashed whippets. Slowly the boat swung round on her rudder to aim. But Towers did not give the word.

His hand had been on the firing lever, his eye on the periscope table and, as the image of the great ship above him swung into view, he suddenly bent forward.

Then—

"Good God!" he whispered between his teeth. "Good God!"

For from the shadow of the big ship up above emerged, clear of the after turret, the jackstaff and the White Ensign.

III

THE SPIRIT MOVES

FINDLAY CAME TO REPORT some ten minutes later.

"I have tested the lighting, lock, stock and barrel," he said. "Man, it's a' pairfect. Yon failure wus juist a contradiction o' a' the laws of pheesics."

It had to go at that.

For the benefit of the crew, Towers put it down to Frillish. Frillish was the only supernumerary. She had come aboard at Nidport with one of the artificers. Calthrop had named her Phyllis; the owner had added Frisky, a concession to her exuberance. It remained for the "Tiffy" responsible for her presence to evolve in a state of rum the soul-satisfying amalgamation. Frillish was an intelligent tabby of three months.

Towers said Frillish must have dug her teeth into a wire and short-circuited. Findlay knew that in that case she would have been a cinder in the thousandth part of a second, but he did not say so. In the Service you are paid to do things, not to prove them.

Anyhow, Frillish carried the guilt of the occasion and was not worried thereby. She was not worried by anything except the captain's state-room. That she hated like the plague. Twice she had been taken in there and each time she had fought a way out, leaving marks of her displeasure on the owner's hands. Not that she disliked Towers; she had a large heart and loved all the crew, so she took her telling-off from the Number 1 tube team with great dignity and forgave them all. Then she went down to the engine room and tried to mesmerise the dynamos.

It was well for the men that they had Frillish, for the brooding spirit of the ship grew more intense as time passed. Findlay spoke to the owner about it once.

"There's something not canny about her, sir."

"Anyway, if it saves us from sinking our own battleships, I don't care what it is," laughed Towers.

But it didn't make for harmony. It got on the nerves in that grey, ice-cold desert of bluff seas where they kept station. It made them do strange things. Once, after an eight hours' vigil, they had gone down for rest and warmth to lie on the mud, when an over-powering desire came to Towers to get to the surface again, to get there at once, to go up and look round at any cost. It was unreasonable; he fought it for half-an-hour, then up he went, wondering what his men would think. A full moon hung in air above them, and as the periscope nosed around to seek for prey it showed a covey of enemy destroyers which had just passed them. If U.C. 07 had been on the surface five minutes earlier they would have been an easy mark.

"There's some sense in this old spook, anyway," said Towers, while he lamented his luck. "Next time you give orders, old sport, we'll make it so."

Then came the affair of the *Cuxhaven*. The moments that U.C. 07 had been freezing for, three weeks beneath the sea, arrived just before sunset of a frosty day. There was no mist and the horizon showed on the table like a silver string dividing gold from grey.

"Smoke, west-sou'-west," was reported from the conning-tower; a moment later, "Smoke, a point south."

Calthrop went up into the look-out.

"Seems that's what we're looking for, sir," said the seaman joyfully.

Calthrop nodded, then sprang down the rail like a cat; this was a matter for the owner.

They proceeded as requisite with extreme care and defined their prey—the fattest spoil that ever good little submarine could desire—three transports, two large cruisers and a screen of destroyers joyfully travelling up the coast to help in the great drive. Every man was at his station, every hand and foot and eye braced and ready in its appointed position, every ear waiting the order for the hand to move. The mere concentration of the men, silent and still, brought sweat out on their faces, though that would never mar the cold precision of their action when the cranks were thrown in and the great machine swung to its fell intent. The men at the course and elevation wheels moved the spokes mechanically while their steadfast eyes never left the indicators. In the conning-tower the owner bent over the table and watched.

The convoy was all about him now; on the port bow was a cruiser, on the starboard the leading transport. Suddenly he passed the signal for the forward port tube and changed course a point to starboard. As she swung round he released the starboard torpedo. Then he dived.

So far he had not been seen. He turned suddenly beneath the water, making for the tail of the convoy, and as he set the ship to rise two dull concussions came to him through the water, rocking the great steel shell in its course. Up he came with his hand on the signal to dive again and his eye already on that part of the black table where the image of his work would appear.

Recalling that moment, Towers says that, however he had regarded that feeling of a strange presence on his ship before, he no longer questioned it then. He knew, long seconds before the periscope screen glowed bright, what he would see, for a voice, inarticulate but plain within his brain, seemed to cry, "That pays for my Utopia." But if those thoughts floated in the subconscious chambers of his brain, his working thoughts was cold and diamond clear.

The screen glowed. A huddled mass in one far rim showed his victims heeling and sagging. Before him and abeam on either side two scared transports wheeled outward, panic-stricken. Swift as thought two more white-tailed avengers sped upon their track. He looked round, swinging the periscope round the skyline, hungry for more prey, and, as he did so, heard a voice that seemed to rise from everywhere in the ship cry heartily—

"Dive, you cross-eyed barnacles!"

He felt the tilt of the ship as someone answered to the call, and he himself, unreasoning, stretched his hand out for the signal lever, but just for a second, before he could touch it, a great triangular wedge invaded the edge of the screen, then the water closed over them, and the periscope was blind. Towers knew that triangle; it was the black bows of a destroyer tearing down to ram.

The water hissed and chattered round them for a second as they dropped, then something jerked them over as it swept screaming by. A moment later and they bumped into mud which held them for a good half-minute; then they swung clear on the bottom, hidden but safe.

As the engines were shut off Towers received his report. "All sound, everywhere!" They came to the conclusion that some deck gear had carried away. (Later they found it was the wireless.)

"Lucky you ordered us to dive, sir," said Calthrop, as they lay at ease with thankful hearts upon the mud.

"Yes," said Towers absently, and a moment later went up into the conning-tower. The depth indicator showing his last order stood at sea level. He went back into his state-room. Frillish lay there curled up and sleeping on the chair!

NOW WHEN TOWERS CAME back to Nidport he sought out a man who knew Dixon and talked about him.

"Was he much of a chap with his tongue?" asked Towers.

"Well," was the answer, "he could curse as well as most masters on the West African route. You have some choice stuff to handle at times there. But Billy Dixon had a strange way of knocking up quaint names that startled his men much more than plain sailor's English."

"As how?" asked Towers.

"Well, he might call 'em lumps of fish-glue, or cross-eyed barnacles," was the answer. "That last was a favourite of his."

That is why Captain Dixon's grave in Nidport cemetery came, six months after his burial there, to be strangely adorned with a glorious wreath—

> "*In grateful memory,*
> *from his shipmates of the U.C. 07.*"

Shipmates? Well, who knows?

COACHWHIP PUBLICATIONS

COACHWHIPBOOKS.COM

BLACK SPIRITS
AND WHITE
RALPH ADAMS CRAM

TALES OF THE
SUPERNATURAL
JAMES PLATT

SHADOWS GOTHIC
AND GROTESQUE

ISBN 1-61646-059-8

INTRODUCTION BY TIM PRASIL

ARTHUR MACHEN

THE DYSON
CHRONICLES

THE INMOST LIGHT · THE SHINING PYRAMID
THE RED HAND · THE THREE IMPOSTORS

ISBN 1-61646-227-2

Coachwhip Publications

CoachwhipBooks.com

HAUNTS &
HORRORS

STRANGE & SUPERNATURAL
FICTION BY M. P. SHIEL

ISBN 1-61646-119-5